ON THE RAZZLE

Also by Tom Stoppard

ON THE RAZZLE

by

TOM STOPPARD

Adapted from
Einen Jux will er sich machen
by
JOHANN NESTROY

FABER AND FABER
London & Boston

First published in 1981
by Faber and Faber Limited
3 Queen Square London WC1N 3AU
Printed in Great Britain by
Latimer Trend & Company Ltd Plymouth
All rights reserved

All rights whatsoever in this play are strictly reserved and professional applications to perform it, etc., must be made in advance, before rehearsals begin, to Fraser and Dunlop (Scripts) Limited of 91 Regent Street, London W1, and amateur applications for permission to perform it, etc., must be made in advance, before rehearsals begin, to Samuel French Limited of 26 Southampton Street, London WC2

British Library Cataloguing in Publication Data

Stoppard, Tom
On the razzle.
I. Title   II. Nestroy, Johann. Jux will er sich
machen.
822/.914   PR6069.T6

ISBN 0–571–11835–6

CHARACTERS

WEINBERL
CHRISTOPHER
SONDERS
MARIE
ZANGLER
GERTRUD
BELGIAN FOREIGNER
MELCHIOR
HUPFER
PHILIPPINE
MADAME KNORR
MRS FISCHER
COACHMAN
WAITER ONE
WAITER TWO
GERMAN MAN
GERMAN WOMAN
SCOTS MAN
SCOTS WOMAN
CONSTABLE
LISETTE
MISS BLUMENBLATT
RAGAMUFFIN

PIPER, CITIZENS, WAITERS, CUSTOMERS, ETC.

On the Razzle opened at the Lyttelton Theatre on 18 September 1981. The cast included:

WEINBERL	Michael Kitchen
CHRISTOPHER	Felicity Kendall
SONDERS	Barry McGinn
ZANGLER	Dinsdale Landen
MADAME KNORR	Sara Kestelman

Directed by Peter Wood
Designed by Carl Toms

INTRODUCTION

On the Razzle is an adaptation of *Einen Jux will er sich machen* by Johann Nestroy (1801–62), who flourished as a comic actor and playwright in Vienna during the 1840s and '50s. Nestroy wrote eighty-odd plays, a handful of which are still regularly performed in that city, while thirty or forty others have had at least one revival in the German-speaking theatre since the Second World War. It is still as a Viennese writing for Viennese that his fame survives, for his eccentric way with language amd his immersion in Viennese dialect gives partial truth to the assertion of one critic that Nestroy is 'untranslatable, even into German'.

This text is not, and could not be, labelled 'a translation'. All the main characters and most of the plot come from Nestroy but almost none of the dialogue attempts to offer a translation of what Nestroy wrote. My method might be compared to cross-country hiking with map and compass, where one takes a bearing on the next landmark and picks one's own way towards it.

Nestroy's way was satirical and verbally outrageous and often turned on a local reference. He also liked to include comic songs between scenes. *On the Razzle* makes no use of dialect, ignores period flavour in dialogue, and has no songs. It is still set in Vienna (though about fifty years later than *Einen Jux*) but not essentially so. The two essentials which this play takes from the original are, firstly, the almost mythic tale of two country mice escaping to town for a day of illicit freedom, adventure, mishap and narrow escapes from discovery; and, secondly, the prime concern to make the tale as comic an entertainment as possible.

Having no German I am indebted to Neville and Stephen Plaice who prepared a close literal translation for me at the request

7

of the National Theatre (and who suggested the title). To Peter Wood, who directed the National Theatre production, is owed the idea of bringing a new version of *Einen Jux* from the Danube to the South Bank.

I say 'new' version because there is already a celebrated old one, Thornton Wilder's *The Matchmaker*. It is not widely known—I didn't know it myself—that Wilder's play and (hence *Hello Dolly!* as well) is an adaptation of *Einen Jux*. When I discovered this I turned to other Nestroy plays thinking that perhaps in bringing a play from this almost unknown comic master into the English theatre I should take a path less famously trod, but I soon returned to *Jux* (its title contracting as affection grew). Firstly, this was the play which Peter Wood most wanted to do, attracted by the mythic quality mentioned above. Secondly, Wilder's temperament, which serves *The Matchmaker* so well, made gentler and more dignified use of the original than I intended, while, furthermore, his adaptation of the plot was rather more free than anything I had in mind. For example Dolly Levi, the matchmaker of the title is Wilder's own invention.

So I offer myself the hope that the differences between the two are at least as great as the similarities, and that *On the Razzle*, if not an absolutely essential addition to the canon of adaptations in English from *Einen Jux will er sich machen*, is at least a welcome one.

TOM STOPPARD

8

ACT ONE

Zangler's shop
In which customers are served with great panache by WEINBERL *and*
CHRISTOPHER. MARIE *is the cashier in a gilded cage. Old-fashioned
spring-loaded canisters travel on wires between the cage and the
counters. A chute delivers a large sack of flour from up above to a
position behind* WEINBERL's *counter. There is a trap door to a cellar.*
SONDERS, *incognito, is among the customers. A town clock chimes the
hour. Customers are being ushered out by* CHRISTOPHER. SONDERS
remains. Shop closing for lunch.

Zangler's room

ZANGLER *and* GERTRUD. ZANGLER *is usually worked up, as now.*
GERTRUD *never is.*

ZANGLER: My tailor has let me down again.

GERTRUD: Yes, I can see.

ZANGLER: No, you damned well can't. I'm referring to my new
uniform which hasn't arrived yet, and today is the grand
annual parade with the massed bands of the Sporting and
Benevolent Societies of the Grocers' Company. It's enough
to make one burst a bratwurst. There I'll be, president-
elect and honorary whipper-in of the Friends of the Opera
Fur and Feather Club, three times winner of the Johann
Strauss Memorial Shield for Wing-shooting, and I'll have
to appear before the public in my old uniform. Perhaps I'd
better not go out at all. That fortune-hunter Sonders is
after my ward.

GERTRUD: My word.

ZANGLER: My ward! If they're not deaf they're dummkopfs!

9

I won't rest easy until Marie is safely out of his reach. Now, don't forget, Marie's luggage is to be sent ahead to my sister-in-law's, Miss Blumenblatt at twenty-three Carlstrasse.

GERTRUD: Miss Blumenblatt's.

ZANGLER: What is the address?

GERTRUD: Twenty-three Carlstrasse.

ZANGLER: What is it?

GERTRUD: Twenty-three Carlstrasse.

ZANGLER: Very well. Marie can stay with her until Sonders finds some other innocent girl to pursue, and furthermore it will stop the little slut from chasing after *him*. I'm damned sure they're sending messages to each other but I can't work out how they're doing it.

(*Zing! In the shop—now closed—a cash-canister zings along the wire to* MARIE *in her gilded cage.*)

Zangler's shop

The shop is closed. WEINBERL *and* CHRISTOPHER *are absent.* SONDERS, *half hidden, has sent the canister.* ZANGLER *is on to him.*

ZANGLER: Sonders!

MARIE: Uncle!

SONDERS: Herr Zangler!

ZANGLER: Unhand my foot, sir!

SONDERS: I love your niece!

ZANGLER: (*Outraged*) My knees, sir? (*Mollified*) Oh, my *niece*. (*Outraged*) Well, my niece and I are not to be prised apart so easily, and nor are hers, I hope I make my meaning clear?

SONDERS: Marie must be mine!

ZANGLER: Never! She is a star out of thy firmament, Sonders! I am a Zangler, provision merchant to the beau-monde, top board for the Cheesemongers and number three in the Twelve Bore Club.

SONDERS: Only three?

ZANGLER: Do you suppose I'd let my airedale be hounded up hill and—my heiress be mounted up hill and bank by a truffle-hound—be trifled with and hounded by a mountebank?! Not for all the tea in China! Well, I might for all the tea in China, or the rice—no, that's ridiculous— the preserved ginger then—no, let's say half the tea, the ginger, a shipment of shark-fin soup double-discounted just to take it off your hands—

SONDERS: All you think about is money!

ZANGLER: All I think about *is* money! As far as I'm concerned any man who molests Marie might as well have his hand in my till!

SONDERS: I make no secret of the fact that I am not the *éminence grise* of Oriental trade, but I have expectations, and no outstanding debts.

(*A man, a* FOREIGNER, *visible in the street, starts knocking on the shop door.* MARIE *has emerged from her cage and goes to deal with it.*)

ZANGLER: We're closed for lunch. What expectations?

FOREIGNER: (*Shouting outside*) Enshuldigen!

ZANGLER: Closed!

FOREIGNER: Mein heren! Ich nicht ein customer . . .

ZANGLER: What did he say?

MARIE: I don't know, Uncle, I think he's a foreigner.

FOREIGNER: Gut morgen—danke shorn.

ZANGLER: We're closed! Open two o'clock!

FOREIGNER: Ich comen looken finden Herr Sonders.

SONDERS: Sonders?

FOREIGNER: Herr Sonders? Ich haben ein document.

ZANGLER: He's a creditor!

SONDERS: (*Panics*) Don't let him in.

FOREIGNER: Herr Sonders!

SONDERS: Nein, nein—I'm busy—

ZANGLER: No debts, eh?

FOREIGNER: Ja—dett!—

SONDERS: Close the door!

(MARIE, *who has opened the door slightly, now closes it and the* FOREIGNER *retires. The* FOREIGNER *is in fact a legal messenger who has come from Belgium to announce the death of* SONDERS's *rich aunt. He succeeds in this endeavour at the end of the play. In recoiling from the* FOREIGNER, SONDERS *has retired through the exit to* ZANGLER'*s room, where the action continues;* MARIE *does not follow.*)

ZANGLER: No debts, eh!

SONDERS: No outstanding debts, I said—run-of-the-mill debts I may have. I probably overlooked my hatter, who is a bit short. But as for my expectations, Herr Zangler, I have the honour to inform you that I have a rich aunt in Brussels.

ZANGLER: A rich aunt in Brussels! I reel, I totter, I am routed from the field! A rich aunt in Brussels—I'm standing here with my buttons undone and he has a rich aunt in Brussels.

SONDERS: She's going to leave me all her money.

ZANGLER: When is that?

SONDERS: When she's dead, of course.

ZANGLER: Listen, I know Brussels. Your auntie will be sitting up in bed in a lace cap when Belgium produces a composer.

SONDERS: I hope so because while she lives I know she'll make me a liberal allowance.

ZANGLER: A liberal allowance!? I'm afraid I never do business on the basis of grandiloquent coinage, and in the lexicon of the false prospectus 'a liberal allowance' is the alpha and oh my God, how many times do I have to tell you?—I will not allow my ward to go off and marry abroad.

SONDERS: Then I'll stay here and marry her, if that's your wont.

ZANGLER: And meanwhile in Brussels your inheritance will be eaten to the bone by codicils letting my wont wait upon her will like the poor cat with the haddock.

SONDERS: The what?

ZANGLER: Look to the aunt! Don't waste your time mooning and skulking around my emporium—I'm sending Marie away to a secret address where you will never find her, search how you will.

(*To* GERTRUD *who has entered with* ZANGLER'*s old uniform.*) What is it?!

GERTRUD: Twenty-three Carlstrasse, Miss Blumenblatt's. Should I let Marie have the new travelling case?

SONDERS: Twenty-three Carlstrasse . . .!

ZANGLER: (*Spluttering*) You old—you stupid—

GERTRUD: Should I let Marie have—

ZANGLER: —old baggage!

GERTRUD: *Not* the new travelling case . . .

SONDERS: (*Leaving*) My humble respects . . .

GERTRUD: Here is your old uniform. And the new servant has arrived.

SONDERS: Your servant, ma'am!

GERTRUD: His.

(SONDERS *goes*.)

ZANGLER: You prattling old fool, who asked you to open your big mouth?

GERTRUD: You're upset. I can tell.

ZANGLER: Where is Marie?

GERTRUD: She's trying on her Scottish travelling coat you got her cheap from your fancy.

ZANGLER: My fancy? My fiancée! A respectable widow and the Madame of 'Madame Knorr's Fashion House'.

GERTRUD: I thought as much—so it's a betrothal.

ZANGLER: No it isn't, damn your nerve, it's a hat and coat shop! Now get out and send in the new servant. And don't let Marie out of your sight. If she and Sonders exchange so much as a glance while I'm gone I'll put you on cabbage-water till you can piss it back into the soup-pot without knowing the difference.

(*Exit* GERTRUD.)

This place is beginning to lose its chic for me. I bestride the mercantile trade of this parish like a colossus, and run a bachelor establishment second to none as far as the eye can see, and I'm surrounded by village idiots and nincompetent poops of every stripe. It's an uphill struggle trying to instil a little tone into this place.

(*There is a knock on the door.*)

Entrez!

(*There is a knock on the door.*)

(*Furiously*) Come in!

(*Enter* MELCHIOR.)

MELCHIOR: Sorry, are you the grocer, your eminence?

ZANGLER: You do me too much honour and not enough. I am Herr Zangler, purveyor of high-class provisions.

MELCHIOR: I understand you are in desperate need of a servant.

ZANGLER: You understand wrong. There's no shortage of rogues like you, only of masters to give them gainful employment.

MELCHIOR: That's classic. And there's something in it. A good servant will keep for years, while masters are being ruined every day. How's business by the way?—don't tell me 'Don't ask'.

ZANGLER: You strike me as rather impertinent.

MELCHIOR: I thought that was shop talk. Please disregard it as the inexperience of youth, as the poet said.

ZANGLER: Do you have a reference?

MELCHIOR: I'm afraid not, I just read it somewhere.

ZANGLER: Have you got a testimonial?

MELCHIOR: (*Producing a tattered paper*) I have, sir. And it's a classic, if I say so myself.

ZANGLER: Is this it? I've never seen anything like it.

MELCHIOR: Thank you.

ZANGLER: 'Honest, industrious, enterprising, intelligent, responsible, cheerful, imaginative, witty, well-spoken, modest, in a word classic . . .'

MELCHIOR: When do you want me to start?

ZANGLER: Just a moment, aren't you forgetting the interview?

MELCHIOR: So I am—how much are you paying?

ZANGLER: Six guilders a month, including laundry.

MELCHIOR: I don't do laundry.

ZANGLER: I mean the housekeeper will wash your shirts.

MELCHIOR: That's classic. I like to be clean.

ZANGLER: And board, of course.

MELCHIOR: Clean and bored.

ZANGLER: And lodging.

MELCHIOR: Clean and bored and lodging—

ZANGLER: All included.

MELCHIOR: Ah, board and lodging. How about sharing a bed?

ZANGLER: I won't countenance immorality.

MELCHIOR: Own bed. As for the board, at my last place it was groaning fit to bust, the neighbours used to bang on the walls.

ZANGLER: I assure you, no one goes hungry here: soup, beef,

14

pudding, all the trimmings.

MELCHIOR: Classic. I always have coffee with my breakfast.

ZANGLER: It has never been the custom here for the servant to have coffee.

MELCHIOR: You wouldn't like me to turn to liquor from the stock?

ZANGLER: Certainly not.

MELCHIOR: Agreed, then.

ZANGLER: What? Well, if you do a good job . . . coffee then.

MELCHIOR: From the pot?

ZANGLER: Ad liberandum.

MELCHIOR: Is that yes or no?

ZANGLER: Yes.

MELCHIOR: Sounds classic.

ZANGLER: Why do you keep using that word? It's stupid.

MELCHIOR: There's nothing stupid about the word, it's just the way some people use it without discrimination. Was there anything else you wanted to ask me?

ZANGLER: No . . . I don't think so.

MELCHIOR: Well, that seems satisfactory. You won't regret this, sir—I have always parted from my employers on the best of terms.

ZANGLER: You have never been sacked?

MELCHIOR: Technically, yes, but only after I have let it be known by subtle neglect of my duties that the job has run its course.

ZANGLER: That's very considerate.

MELCHIOR: I don't like to give offence by giving notice—in a servant it looks presumptuous.

ZANGLER: That shows modesty.

MELCHIOR: Your humble servant, sir.

ZANGLER: Yes, all right.

MELCHIOR: Classic!

ZANGLER: Only you'll have to stop using that word.

MELCHIOR: C-count on it. What are my duties?

ZANGLER: Your duties are the duties of a servant. To begin with you can help me finish dressing—and if that tailor shows his face tell him to go to hell.

15

(*Enter tailor,* HUPFER. HUPFER *brings with him* ZANGLER'S *new uniform on a tailor's dummy. The complete rig-out includes a ridiculous hat with feathers etc., polished riding boots with monstrous shining and very audible spurs, and the uniform itself which is top heavy with gold buttons and braid etc. Leather strapping supports holsters for knife, gun, sword . . . The general effect is sporting and musical. The new uniform is brighter than the old, which is bright. The tailor is only responsible for the clothes. The rest of the stuff is already in the room.*)

HUPFER: Here we are—the masterpiece is ready.

ZANGLER: You managed it, my dear Hupfer! In the nick of time.

MELCHIOR: Go to hell.

HUPFER: Eh, what?

ZANGLER: Shut up!

MELCHIOR: (*To the dummy*) Shut up!

HUPFER: Well, with the help of two journeyman tailors I have done the impossible—here—let me help you into it.

MELCHIOR: I worked for a tailor once. I cooked his goose for him.

HUPFER: There we are.

MELCHIOR: Everything went well until I got confused and goosed his cook.

ZANGLER: Pay attention. You may learn something.

MELCHIOR: After that he got a valet stand.

ZANGLER: You'll see how a uniform should fit . . . except it's a bit tight isn't it?

(*It is more than a bit tight.*)

HUPFER: Snug.

ZANGLER: It's somewhat constricted, surely.

HUPFER: That's the style.

ZANGLER: But it's cutting me under the arms, the buttons will fly off when I sit down, and I can't breathe.

HUPFER: It's a uniform, it is not supposed to be a nightshirt.

ZANGLER: How do I look?

MELCHIOR: I'd rather not say.

ZANGLER: I order you! How do I look?

MELCHIOR: Classic.

ZANGLER: (*Triumphantly*) You see!

HUPFER: (*Baffled*) Classic?

ZANGLER: I don't understand it. You took my measurements.

MELCHIOR: That explains it. If God had been a tailor there'd be seven and a half furlongs to the mile and the world would look like a three-cornered hat . . .

HUPFER: All right! It'll be ready Thursday!

MELCHIOR: And he would have promised it for Thursday . . . We'd all have been on a five-day week.

ZANGLER: Shut up.

MELCHIOR: (*To* HUPFER) Shut up.

HUPFER: You dare to let your servant speak to me like that?

MELCHIOR: In the livery of the Zanglers I am no man's minion.

ZANGLER: That's well said. What's your name?

MELCHIOR: Melchior.

ZANGLER: Melchior, throw this man out.

HUPFER: Don't touch me! You, sir, received your measurements from nature. The tailor's art is to interpret them to your best advantage, and move the buttons later. My humble respects. I will leave my bill.

MELCHIOR: (*Thrusting the dummy at* HUPFER) Oh no you won't— you'll take him with you!

(*Exit* HUPFER *with dummy.*)

What should I do next?

ZANGLER: There's a coach leaving for town in five minutes. I want you to be on it.

MELCHIOR: It's been a pleasure. I usually get a week's money.

ZANGLER: No, no, my dear fellow, I want you to go to town and engage a private room at the Black and White Chop House. Order a good dinner for two and wait for me there.

MELCHIOR: Dinner for two, wait for you there.

ZANGLER: Tell them it's a celebration—foaming tankards—cold meats—pickles—potato salad—plum dumplings . . .

MELCHIOR: You'll spoil me.

ZANGLER: It's not for you. I'm entertaining my fiancée.

MELCHIOR: A previous engagement? My congratulations, Herr Zangler.

ZANGLER: Thank you. She's the Madame of Madame Knorr's

Fashion House. You may know it.

MELCHIOR: No, but I think I know the piano player.

ZANGLER: It's a hat shop in Annagasse. Of course she's a millineress in her own right.

MELCHIOR: Enough said. And the shop on top.

ZANGLER: No, she's on top of the shop. What are you talking about?

MELCHIOR: I don't know.

ZANGLER: I'm going to take her to dinner and name the day. You can expect me after the parade.

MELCHIOR: Are we travelling together?

ZANGLER: No, I can't be in a hurry, I'm having trouble with my niece.

MELCHIOR: It's the trousers.

ZANGLER: No, it's Sonders, the Casanova incarnate. Marie is very vulnerable. If she so much as sets foot outside the door she's going to catch it from me.

MELCHIOR: How long have you had it?

ZANGLER: No. I mean the Don Juan.

MELCHIOR: Has he had it?

ZANGLER: I don't think so. She's in her room trying on her Scottish coat.

MELCHIOR: I'll work it out later.

ZANGLER: After all I am her uncle.

MELCHIOR: I've worked it out.

ZANGLER: Now here's some money to catch the coach.

MELCHIOR: Can't I meet the rest of your staff?

ZANGLER: There isn't time. Do you understand my requirements?

MELCHIOR: Perfectly.

ZANGLER: Repeat them.

MELCHIOR: Catch the coach—go straight to the Imperial Gardens Café—private dinner for two, champagne on ice . . .

ZANGLER: No—no—no—the Black and White Chop House!

MELCHIOR: Sir, I beg you to consider. Madame Knorr is a woman of the world, sophisticated, dressed to the nines with a hat to knock your eye out and an eye to knock your hat off. You want to wine her, dine her and name the day. Now does that suggest to you a foaming tankard and a plate

18

of cold cuts in the old Black and White?

ZANGLER: (*Slightly puzzled*) Yes it does. What are you getting at?

MELCHIOR: Madame Knorr is not just another hausfrau. Fashion is her middle name.

ZANGLER: More or less. Knorr Fashion House. I think I see what you mean . . . The Imperial Gardens Café is a fashionable place, is it?

MELCHIOR: It's the only place for the quality at the moment.

ZANGLER: The quality . . . Are you sure it is quite refined?

MELCHIOR: Refined?! The ploughman's lunch is six oysters and a nectarine.

ZANGLER: I see . . . well, perhaps just this once.

MELCHIOR: Leave it to me, sir—champagne—lobster—roast fowl—fruit ices—desserts.

ZANGLER: Pickles—dumplings—

MELCHIOR: And to finish off, to get her in the mood—

ZANGLER: Perhaps we should have—

MELCHIOR: ⎱
ZANGLER: ⎰ (*Together*) A nice bottle of the hard stuff.

MELCHIOR: (*Leaving*) Schnapps!

(*Coach horn.* ZANGLER *now puts on the rest of his outfit, boots, hat, etc.*)

ZANGLER: Well, that seems all right. Just the ticket. First class. Why do I have a sense of impending disaster? (*He reflects.*) Sonders is after my niece and has discovered the secret address where I am sending her to the safe keeping of my sister-in-law Miss Blumenblatt, who has never laid eyes on him, or, for that matter, on Marie either since she was a baby—while I have to leave my business in the charge of my assistant and an apprentice, and follow my new servant, whom I haven't had time to introduce to anyone, to town so that I can join the parade in a uniform I can't sit down in and take my fiancée to dinner in a fashionable restaurant.

One false move and we could have a farce on our hands.

Zangler's shop
The shop is closed for lunch. WEINBERL *occupies it like a gentleman of
leisure. He is writing a letter at the counter. He has a cigar and a glass
of wine.* CHRISTOPHER *is at the door leading to the rest of the house.
He is holding a broom, the Cinderella-type of broom, not a yard broom.*

CHRISTOPHER: He's gone.

(*He joins* WEINBERL *and is offered a glass. There is also a jar
of rollmops to hand.*)

Ah, thank you, Mr Weinberl.

(WEINBERL *continues to write. At* CHRISTOPHER'*s position on
the counter there is a stack of torn pages from newspapers used
here for wrapping purposes.* CHRISTOPHER *leans on the stack,
reading the top page.*)

Aha, I thought so . . . cocoa is up six points.

WEINBERL: (*Without looking up*) When was that?

CHRISTOPHER: (*Examining the top of the page*) Week before last.

(WEINBERL *signs his letter and blots it.*)

WEINBERL: Does it ever occur to you, Christopher, that we're the
backbone of this country?

CHRISTOPHER: You and me, Mr Weinberl?

WEINBERL: The merchant class.

CHRISTOPHER: Ah yes.

WEINBERL: The backbone of the country. The very vertebrae of
continental stability. From coccyx to clavicle—from the
Carpathians to . . . where you will . . .

CHRISTOPHER: The toe-nails . . .

WEINBERL: . . . the Tyrol, from Austro to breakfast, and
Hungaria to lights out, the merchant class is the backbone
of the empire on which the sun shines out of our doings;
do you ever say that to yourself?

CHRISTOPHER: Not in so many words, Mr Weinberl.

WEINBERL (*Pulling* CHRISTOPHER'*s forelock*) Well you should.
What is it after all that distinguishes man from beast?

CHRISTOPHER: Not a lot, Mr Weinberl.

WEINBERL: Trade.

CHRISTOPHER: I was thinking that.

WEINBERL: What would we be without trade?

CHRISTOPHER: Closed, Mr Weinberl.

WEINBERL: That's it. The shutters would go up on civilization as we know it. It's the merchant class that holds everything together. Uniting the deep-sea fisherman and the village maiden over a pickled herring on a mahogany counter . . .

CHRISTOPHER: You've put me right off me rollmop.

(*He has been eating one.*)

WEINBERL: . . . uniting the hovels of Havana to the House of Hanover over a box of hand-rolled cigars, and the matchgirl to the church warden in the fall of a lucifer. The pearl fisher and the courtesan are joined at the neck by the merchant class. We are the brokers between invention and necessity, balancing supply and demand on the knife edge of profit and loss. I give you—the merchant class!

CHRISTOPHER: The merchant class!

(*They toast.*)

WEINBERL: We know good times and we know bad. Sometimes trade stumbles on its march. The great machine seems to hesitate, the whirling cogwheels and reciprocating pistons disengage, an unearthly silence descends upon the mercantile world . . . We sit here idly twisting paper into cones, flicking a duster over piles of preserved figs and pyramids of uncertain dates, swatting flies like wanton gods off the north face of the Emmental, and gazing into the street.

And then suddenly with a great roar the engine bursts into life, and the teeming world of commerce is upon us! Someone wants a pound of coffee, someone else an ounce of capers, *he* wants smoked eel, *she* wants lemons, a skivvy wants rosewater, a fat lady wants butter, but a skinny one wants whalebones, the curate comes for a candy stick, the bailiff roars for a bottle of brandy, and there's a Gadarene rush on the pigs' trotters. At such times the merchant class stands alone, ordering the tumult of desire into the ledgerly rhythm of exchange with a composure as implacable as a cottage loaf. Tongue.

(*During the speech* WEINBERL *has folded his letter and put it in an envelope.* CHRISTOPHER *sticks out his tongue and* WEINBERL *dabs a postage stamp on the tongue and slaps it on the envelope. He seals the envelope with satisfaction.*)

CHRISTOPHER: How is your romance, Herr Weinberl?

WEINBERL: As well as can be expected of a relationship based on pseudonymous correspondence between two post office boxes. One has to proceed cautiously with lonely hearts advertisements. There is a great deal of self-delusion among these women—although I must admit I am becoming very taken with Elegant And Under Forty. I am thinking of coming out from behind my nom de plume of Scaramouche. The trouble is, I rather think I have given her the impression that I am more or less the owner of this place, not to mention others like it . . .

CHRISTOPHER: At least you're not a dogsbody like me.

WEINBERL: Christopher, Christopher, have a pretzel . . . The dignity of labour embraces servant and master, for every master is a servant too, answerable to the voice of a higher authority.

ZANGLER: (*Outside*) Weinberl!

(*Without seeming to hurry* WEINBERL *instantly puts things to order.*)

WEINBERL: I thought you said he'd gone.

CHRISTOPHER: He must have changed his mind.

(ZANGLER *enters from the house.*)

ZANGLER: Ah, there you are. Is it time to open the shop?

WEINBERL: Not quite, Chief. I was just getting everything straight.

ZANGLER: What about this pretzel?

WEINBERL: The pretzel defeated me completely. (*To* CHRISTOPHER.) Put it back. Are you going to the parade, Herr Zangler?

ZANGLER: No, I'm going beagling. What do you think?

WEINBERL: I think you're making fun of me, Chief.

ZANGLER: How does it look?

WEINBERL: (*Tactfully*) Snug.

ZANGLER: Do you think it should be let out?

WEINBERL: Not till after dark.

ZANGLER: What?

WEINBERL: No.

ZANGLER: Are you sure?

22

WEINBERL: I like it, Chief.

CHRISTOPHER: I like it.

ZANGLER: I can't deny it's smart. Did you notice the spurs?

(*The spurs announce themselves every time* ZANGLER *moves.*)

WEINBERL: The spurs? Oh yes . . .

CHRISTOPHER: I noticed them.

ZANGLER: I'm rather pleased with the effect. I feel like the cake
of the week.

WEINBERL: That's very well put, Chief.

ZANGLER: I don't mean the cake of the week—

WEINBERL: Not the cake of the week—the Sheikh of Kuwait—
no—

ZANGLER: No—

CHRISTOPHER: The clerk of the works—

ZANGLER: No!

WEINBERL: The cock of the walk?

ZANGLER: That's the boy.

WEINBERL: You'll be the cock of the walk, Chief, the pride of
the Sporting and Benevolent Musical Fusiliers of the
Grocers' Company, and what wonderful work they do for
the widows and orphans.

ZANGLER: I was just setting off when I suddenly had doubts.

WEINBERL: I assure you, without people like the grocers there'd
be no widows and orphans at all.

ZANGLER: No, I mean I had doubts about leaving.

WEINBERL: I don't understand you, Chief.

ZANGLER: My niece and ward is preying on my mind. There's
something not quite right there.

CHRISTOPHER: My niece and ward *are* preying on my mind—?

ZANGLER: (*Ignoring him*) Something not quite the ticket. Sonders
is a dyed-in-the-wool Don Juan. He's turned Marie's head
and for all I know she's already lost it.

WEINBERL: Well, she didn't lose it in shop-hours.

ZANGLER: I'm going to frustrate him.

WEINBERL: Frustration is too good for him, Chief.

ZANGLER: I'm sending Marie away for a few days. You'll have to
manage the while the till . . . No—

WEINBERL: To while the time . . .

23

ZANGLER: No!

WEINBERL: The till the while?

ZANGLER: That's the boy. You'll have to manage the till the while, and do the books at the close of business. I suppose you're prepared to do that?

WEINBERL: Very well prepared if I may say so, Herr Zangler.

ZANGLER: There will be other changes. Prepare yourself for a surprise. I have always prided myself on being a good master who has made every reasonable provision for his staff.

WEINBERL: You have, Chief.

ZANGLER: Well, what would you say to having a mistress?

CHRISTOPHER: One each or sharing?

WEINBERL: Congratulations, Chief! We wish you and your bride every happiness.

ZANGLER: Thank you, thank you.

WEINBERL: May one ask who is the fortunate young lady?

ZANGLER: Actually she's a widow, in business like me. Well not actually like me, far from it, it's a haute couture house employing three girls and catering exclusively to the beau-monde. What do you say to that?

WEINBERL: Let him who is without sin cast the first stone.

ZANGLER: What the devil is the matter with everybody! That's another thing that was worrying me—leaving the place in charge of you two. I need someone with a proper sense of responsibility, not a log-rolling counter-clerk and a cack-handed apprentice.

WEINBERL: I'm mortified.

CHRISTOPHER: I'm articled.

WEINBERL: Who have you got in mind, Chief?

ZANGLER: Well, you two of course!

WEINBERL: I mean to put in charge with a sense of responsibility?

ZANGLER: What would you do in my shoes?

WEINBERL: Jingle.

ZANGLER: What?

WEINBERL: Jingle make any difference just for one afternoon, Chief?

ZANGLER: It may be longer. The duration of my absence will

depend on how things go at a certain engagement I have this evening. Meanwhile desperate situations call for desperate measures. Master Christopher! Approach!

CHRISTOPHER: He called me Master. Is it the sack?

ZANGLER: I've been paying for your clothes all these years, as you know.

CHRISTOPHER: No, I thought you bought them outright when you took me on.

WEINBERL: Shut up.

ZANGLER: By rights you owe me another six months' apprenticeship, but to commemorate my nuptials I have decided to forgo those months. I am appointing you chief sales assistant.

WEINBERL: Show your gratitude, then. He's stunned, Chief.

CHRISTOPHER: Chief sales assistant! Oh, Herr Zangler, your bountifulness!

ZANGLER: You may call me Chief. Stop snivelling—where's your—

CHRISTOPHER: Thank you, Chief!

ZANGLER: Thank-you-Chief—no, no—

WEINBERL (*Worried*) Hang on, Chief—

ZANGLER: Hang-on-Chief—no!—

WEINBERL: Aren't I chief sales assistant?

CHRISTOPHER: Will I have my ceremony, Chief? I've got to have my—

ZANGLER: What?

CHRISTOPHER: Initiation, Chief!

ZANGLER: Bless you. And we must have the ceremony. Raise your right trouser and repeat after me . . . I swear.

CHRISTOPHER: I swear . . .

ZANGLER: Weinberl, do you remember how it goes?

WEINBERL: To strive and to abide.

CHRISTOPHER: To strive and to abide.

WEINBERL: No—I swear by the sacred apron of the Grand Victualler—no—it's been a long time . . .

CHRISTOPHER: (*Rapidly*) I swear by the sacred apron of the Imperial Grand Grocer and by the grocery chain of his office, to strive for his victualler in freehold, to abide by his

25

argument which flows from his premises, to honour his custom, keep up his stock, give credit to few, be credit to all, and not be found wanting when weighed in the scales, so help me God!

ZANGLER: You may jump the counter.

(CHRISTOPHER *jumps.*)

That's that. I will inform you of any changes in your duties should any occur to me—except of course that you have to buy your own clothes.

CHRISTOPHER: Thank you, Chief!

ZANGLER: And remember, always give people their change between finger and thumb. Nothing lets down the tone of a place so much as change from the fist.

CHRISTOPHER: Right, Chief.

WEINBERL: Excuse me, Chief. Am I your chief sales assistant or am I not?

ZANGLER: You are not. I have decided to make you my partner. To take effect from the day of my marriage.

WEINBERL: (*Stunned*) Me? Your partner?

ZANGLER: Yes. As a married man who has come into possession of a couture establishment I will be spending more time away from here. It's only right that you should have an interest in the prosperity of the business, and probably cheaper.

WEINBERL: Partner . . .

ZANGLER: Yes, yes, as soon as my bride has consummated my expansion into her turnover you will be my partner. Now—what shall I do? Shall I go or what?

WEINBERL: What . . . ?

ZANGLER: No, I'll go. I'll be back late tonight or possibly next week. It all depends on dinner. (ZANGLER *goes.*)

WEINBERL: (*In a daze*) Partner . . . partner . . . I'm a partner. One moment a put-upon counter-clerk, the next a pillar of the continental trading community.

CHRISTOPHER: Chief sales assistant . . . I've always been at the bottom of the ladder and now . . . (*A thought strikes him.*) Who's going to be under me, then?

WEINBERL: Book-keeper—that was the Himalaya of my

26

aspirations, but from the vantage point of partnership I look tolerantly down upon the book-keeper's place as if from a throne of clouds.

CHRISTOPHER: You're a partner and I'm the entire staff. I'll have two lord-high masters instead of one, three counting the widow, and the weight of my authority will be felt by the housekeeper's cat.

WEINBERL: And yet—strangely enough—now, now of all times, when fortune has smiled upon me like a lunatic upon a worm in an apple, I feel a sense of . . . (*Pause*) grief.

CHRISTOPHER: That cat is going to wish it had never been born.

WEINBERL: What is happening to me? I feel a loosening of obscure restraints . . . Desires stir in my breast like shifting crates on a badly loaded barrow.

CHRISTOPHER: (*Breaks out*) Oh, Mother, what is the wherefore of it all?!—Whither the striving and how the abiding for a poor boy in the grocery trade? I'm glad she's dead and doesn't see me chained to this counter like a dog to a kennel, knowing nothing of the world except what happens to get wrapped around the next pound of groceries. Seeing the sunrise only from an attic window, and the sunset reflected in a row of spice jars, agog at travellers' tales of paved streets! Oh, Mr Weinberl, I have come into my kingdom and I see that it is the locked room from which you celebrate your escape! And if I have to wait until I am as old as you, *that's longer than I've been alive!*

WEINBERL: (*Soberly*) Beyond the door is another room. The servant is the slave of his master and the master is the slave of his business. If only I could look back on a day when I was fancy free, a real razzle of a day packed with adventure and high jinks, a day to remember when I am a grand-grocer with half a yard of watch chain, passing the grog and spinning the yarn with the merchant princes of the retail trade, when I could say, 'Oh, I was a gay dog in my day, a real rapscallion—why, I remember once . . .' but I have nothing to remember.

(*Desperately*) I've got to acquire a past before it's too late!

CHRISTOPHER: Can I come with you, Mr Weinberl?

WEINBERL: Come with me where?

CHRISTOPHER: I want it now!

WEINBERL: Now?

CHRISTOPHER: This very minute!

WEINBERL: (*Appalled*) What? Lock up the shop?

CHRISTOPHER: It's already locked.

WEINBERL: While he's at the parade . . .?

CHRISTOPHER: And dinner in town. It's only us two. Marie is confined to quarters. He'll never know.

WEINBERL: Wait . . . (*He paces about feverishly and then embraces* CHRISTOPHER.) We'll stop the clocks!

CHRISTOPHER: Yes! What?

(WEINBERL *mimics* ZANGLER *and* CHRISTOPHER *mimics* WEINBERL.)

WEINBERL: No—I mean—

CHRISTOPHER: Box the stock—

WEINBERL: No—

CHRISTOPHER: No—bake the cake—no—

WEINBERL: No!

CHRISTOPHER: Cook the books—

WEINBERL: That's the boy—we'll cook the books and blow the cook!

CHRISTOPHER: (*As himself, alarmed*) The cook!

WEINBERL: (*As himself*) The cook!

CHRISTOPHER: Fix the cook!

WEINBERL: Get her in here—no—wait—in here—

(*Into the room, where* ZANGLER's *old uniform is where he left it.* WEINBERL *puts on the trousers and the boots and plays the* GERTRUD *scene with his head stuck into the tunic and his hands half in the sleeves, apparently struggling to pull the garment over his head but not succeeding. Meanwhile—*)

Tell her to tell him I don't want to open the shop—

CHRISTOPHER: Tell her to tell who who doesn't?

WEINBERL: To tell *me he* doesn't—get it?

CHRISTOPHER: Got it!

(CHRISTOPHER *seizes a hand bell and rings it vigorously until* GERTRUD *appears.*)

GERTRUD: So you're still in two minds are you?

28

CHRISTOPHER: He is, and he's half out of both of them.
  (*To* WEINBERL *loudly*.) It's Gertrud, Herr Zangler!
  (*All* WEINBERL'S *lines are muffled and unintelligible and furious.* WEINBERL *speaks*.)
GERTRUD: Twenty-three Carlstrasse, Miss Blumenblatt's.
  (*This is the wrong answer and* WEINBERL *speaks even more furiously*.)
CHRISTOPHER: The master says to tell Mr Weinberl—
  (GERTRUD *is too close*.)
  Stand back—the master says keep your distance or you'll catch it.
GERTRUD: Has he got it too?
  (WEINBERL *again*.)
CHRISTOPHER: The master says tell Mr Weinberl not to open the shop this afternoon.
  (WEINBERL *again*.)
  Is that clear?
GERTRUD: No.
CHRISTOPHER: The master says—
GERTRUD: Yes, I heard you. Don't open the shop. Tell Mr Weinberl.
  (WEINBERL *again*.)
CHRISTOPHER: Strict orders, he says, and now would you be so good as to leave him.
GERTRUD: That doesn't sound like him.
  (WEINBERL *dances about and roars*. CHRISTOPHER *goes as though to help him into the tunic.* GERTRUD *speaks as she leaves*.)
  That's more like him.
CHRISTOPHER: (*Pulling the tunic over* WEINBERL'S *head*) She's gone.
WEINBERL: Now if Zangler finds out about the shop we'll only be following instructions, and Gertrud will have to back up our story.
CHRISTOPHER: I think you'll do very well as a partner.
WEINBERL: He'll think her brains are addled.
CHRISTOPHER: She can't complain. Up to now he thought she didn't have any.

29

WEINBERL: And now, best foot forward.

CHRISTOPHER: I'll get my worsted stocking.

WEINBERL: Is that necessary?

CHRISTOPHER: It's got my savings in it.

WEINBERL: I'll get mine and we'll be off.

(Door slam and jingle of spurs.)

God in heaven he's back again!

(CHRISTOPHER picks up WEINBERL's discarded clothes and runs off towards the shop. Spurs however still approach.)

I can't let him see me like this!

(Before WEINBERL can follow CHRISTOPHER, GERTRUD enters from the kitchen and WEINBERL dives behind the furniture. ZANGLER enters at the same time.)

ZANGLER: *(Shouts)* Marie! Damn and blast it, that swinehound Sonders is nowhere to be seen in the village, and he didn't leave on the coach and Marie's window is open! God in Himalayas!—If I keep having to come back I'll miss the parade. I told you not to let Marie out of your sight.

GERTRUD: You told me to find Weinberl and tell him—

ZANGLER: Don't tell me what I told you—search her room, perhaps he's got my ward's behind between his knees and raped her backwards—no—

GERTRUD: —got back behind your niece and ward's drapes—

ZANGLER: No!

GERTRUD: Got behind your back and in your niece's wardrobe.

ZANGLER: That's the boy. I'll keep watch in the garden if I can find a place to hide.

GERTRUD: Stand in the herbaceous border.

(They leave in different directions. WEINBERL comes out from behind the furniture and runs into the shop, looking for his clothes.)

Zangler's shop

WEINBERL *enters, calling for* CHRISTOPHER. *But he has only just entered when the trap door in the floor starts coming up and he dives into a cupboard.* SONDERS *and* MARIE, *dressed in a voluminous,*

30

tartan, hooded cape, emerge from the cellar.

SONDERS: It's all right, it's deserted—courage, my darling—

MARIE: Oh, August—we mustn't—it isn't proper.

SONDERS: Now's our chance—we can escape by the shop door while they're searching round the back.

MARIE: Oh, but it isn't proper.

SONDERS: Don't you love me?

MARIE: You know I love you but I don't want to run away—

SONDERS: Elopement isn't running away, it's running towards.

MARIE: It isn't proper.

SONDERS: Is it proper for your guardian to behave as if he owns you?

MARIE: Yes. That's why they call it property. I think. Oh, August, you're a terrible man, kiss me again. You made me feel all funny down there.

(He embraces her, more inside her cape than out.)

SONDERS: Oh, Marie!

MARIE: I mean in the cellar—Oh, somebody's coming!

SONDERS: Hide in here!

MARIE: No, it isn't prop—!

(He dives into WEINBERL's cupboard, pulling her after him. CHRISTOPHER enters from a second door with WEINBERL's clothes, calling for him and running out of the shop. The cupboard door bursts open. MARIE comes out, SONDERS comes out and WEINBERL's legs come out. WEINBERL is lying on his front.)

SONDERS: Someone has been eavesdropping on us—

MARIE: I thought it was a squash in there.

SONDERS: If it's that apprentice I'll box his ears and post them to him.

(SONDERS drags WEINBERL out by his heels, or spurs. He and MARIE are aghast to find that ZANGLER seems to be lying on the floor with his face still in the cupboard. SONDERS and MARIE kneel down and bow their heads as WEINBERL gets unsteadily to his feet. WEINBERL gazes down on to the crowns of their heads.)

MARIE: Oh, my uncle!

SONDERS: Oh, my God—Herr Zangler!

31

MARIE: Don't be angry, dear Uncle, I meant no harm.

SONDERS: She's blameless, sir, intact I swear, I mean in fact I swear she did it against her will.

MARIE: I *didn't* do it!

SONDERS: No she didn't—I haven't—Oh, sir, it was love that drove us to deceive you!

(*They are kissing* WEINBERL'*s hands.*)

MARIE: Won't you speak to me, Uncle? Your harshest words are easier to bear than the silence of your anger.

(WEINBERL, *deeply embarrassed, disengages his hands and pats the two heads.*)

SONDERS: What do you . . .?

MARIE: Do you mean . . .?

(*They try to raise their heads but* WEINBERL *firmly keeps their heads down and presses them together.*)

SONDERS: He's blessing our union.

(WEINBERL *guides their faces into a lingering kiss during which he is able to retire, silently, from the room.*)

SONDERS: Marie!

MARIE: Oh, August!

Oh, Uncle, you've made me so . . . Where has he gone?

SONDERS: What a surprising man he is! Beneath his rough manners he is the very soul of tact.

MARIE: (*Getting up*) I always knew he was shy underneath.

SONDERS: Let me kiss you again.

MARIE: You can kiss me properly now!

(*They go into another lingering kiss, during which* ZANGLER *enters. He has a silent apoplexy. At length* SONDERS *notices him.*)

SONDERS: (*Suavely*) Ah, there you are, my dear sir, we were wondering where you'd got to.

ZANGLER: (*Strangled*) Sonders! (*A couple of buttons fly off his uniform.*)

MARIE: Oh, you must call him August now—you're going to be such friends—isn't he handsome?

ZANGLER: I'll kill him.

MARIE: Uncle, but you just—

ZANGLER: Slut!

SONDERS: My dear sir, what can have happened?

ZANGLER: You blackguard! You barefaced dastardly—

SONDERS: He's mad.

ZANGLER: Get out!

(GERTRUD *enters.*)

GERTRUD: (*Placidly*) Oh, you've found them.

MARIE: Oh, Uncle, you're not yourself . . .

ZANGLER: I'll teach you to get up to your coquetry you
meretrix!

GERTRUD: Up to your merry tricks, you coquette . . .

ZANGLER: (*Screams*) Shut up!

MARIE: Oh . . . (*She runs weeping from the room.*)

SONDERS: Marie! . . . This is absurd—I'll come back when
you're feeling calmer.

(ZANGLER, *followed by* GERTRUD, *chases* SONDERS *out.*)

ZANGLER: You dare to show your nose in here again and I'll
cut off your coquette to spite your face! And furthermore
I'll disinherit her!

(*This takes* ZANGLER *and* GERTRUD *out of the room.* WEINBERL,
in his own clothes, and CHRISTOPHER *reappear. They are
gleeful.*)

CHRISTOPHER: Did you hear that?

WEINBERL: Oh my! I feel like a rapscallion. I feel I'm getting a
past at last. Just wait until we really get into our stride.

CHRISTOPHER: Wait!

(CHRISTOPHER *rummages around under the counter and comes
up with a wooden sign saying 'Boy Wanted'. He blows a
prodigious amount of dust off it and hangs it in the window
while* WEINBERL *removes a couple of hats from the hook
behind the door. He passes one hat to* CHRISTOPHER *and they
leave.*)

Arriving in Vienna . . . gaiety and music . . . CHRISTOPHER *takes it all
in wide-eyed. The dialogue is part of the set change.*

CHRISTOPHER: Is the city always like this, Mr Weinberl? All this
gay panoply . . .

WEINBERL: (*Slightly puzzled*) Well . . . more or less . . . it's some time since I . . .

CHRISTOPHER: (*Enthusiastically*) Bands playing—streets full of colourful costumes—it's like a great parade . . .

WEINBERL: (*Thoughtfully*) Yes . . .

CHRISTOPHER: What would old Zangler think if he saw us now?

WEINBERL: Oh yes . . .!
(*The penny drops.*)
Parade?!

CHRISTOPHER: Parade!
(*The parade is going right by them.*)

WEINBERL: My God, suppose Zangler happens to—
(WEINBERL *and* CHRISTOPHER *obviously see* ZANGLER *approaching. The parade music suddenly incorporates the massed spurs of the Grocers' Company.*)
Turn your back—get off the boulevard!

CHRISTOPHER: This way—up the side street!

Annagasse exterior—Madame Knorr's Fashion House
Distant parade. CHRISTOPHER *and* WEINBERL *enter running. They come to a breathless halt outside the windows which flank the entrance door of the fashion house. Windows above.*

CHRISTOPHER: Well, we *nearly* had an adventure.

WEINBERL: It *would* have been our final fling if Zangler had caught sight of us.

CHRISTOPHER: All the same, after three hours in a farm cart and probably six hours trek to get back home, to end up flingless . . .

WEINBERL: Dishonoured and unflung . . . Let's sit down a minute.

CHRISTOPHER: You're not downhearted, are you?

WEINBERL: I don't know. I've been getting a sharp stabbing pain just here.

CHRISTOPHER: You've got the stitch.

WEINBERL: I don't think so. It only happens when I see an open grocer's shop. It'll be just my luck if I've got Weinberl's Disease.

34

CHRISTOPHER: It would certainly be a coincidence. Still, it sounds like the sort of thing people come to Vienna for from all over the world, so to get it while you're here on a rare visit smacks of outrageous good fortune. I'm trying to make you look on the bright side.

WEINBERL: Christopher.

CHRISTOPHER: Yes, Mr Weinberl?

WEINBERL: Embrace me.

(*They embrace.*)

(*Enthusiastically*) There's plenty of time. There's probably an adventure lying in wait for us at this very spot.

(PHILIPPINE *is seen moving inside the shop. She is putting on the lights, since the afternoon is drawing on. The light illuminates, for the first time, the words 'Knorr's Fashion House'.*)

WEINBERL: For all we know we have made an appointment with destiny.

CHRISTOPHER: Nothing is going to happen to us in a poky little street like this.

WEINBERL: That's where you're wrong. It's in the side streets where lurks romance! I've often read about it. Remember 'The Mystery of the Blind Alley'? . . . 'letting his horse have its head, he found himself, without knowing how, in a narrow secluded lane. He noticed a man in a black hat who, he could have sworn, winked at him as he went by. In the same moment he noticed a second man in a dark muffler who, he was almost sure, nudged him as he brushed past. He grasped the reins, undecided whether to follow the man who gave him a nudge or the man who gave him a wink. Suddenly he realized the horse was blind. There was a hint of rain in the air. Without warning, a window above his head was flung open and a dainty female hand . . .'

(*A window is flung open above his head and a dainty female hand empties half a mug of beer into the street.* WEINBERL *and* CHRISTOPHER *leap aside as the window slams shut.*)

WEINBERL: Peasant!

CHRISTOPHER: Critic!

WEINBERL: Architect!

CHRISTOPHER: What sort of riffraff live in this place?

WEINBERL: (*Reading the sign*) Fashion House.

CHRISTOPHER: Moravians, I shouldn't wonder. Arty types. The great unwashed.

WEINBERL: Bohemians.

CHRISTOPHER: We got a bit splashed. You don't think it was . . .?

WEINBERL: I looked too late. How are your powers of observation?

CHRISTOPHER: It all happened so quickly.

(WEINBERL *takes off his hat carefully and dips a finger into the little puddle in its crown. He licks his finger.*)

WEINBERL: It's all right—only a drop of beer. Not a bad beer at that. (*Offers his hat.*)

CHRISTOPHER: Really? (*He dips his finger into* WEINBERL's *hat and licks it.*) So it is.

(WEINBERL *watches this closely.*)

WEINBERL: Lucky.

CHRISTOPHER: Yes, you took a bit of a chance.

WEINBERL: No, I dipped *this* finger but I licked that one. Frankly your powers of observation leave a lot to be desired.

CHRISTOPHER: You'll definitely do very well as a partner.

WEINBERL: It's all quiet. The parade must be over. Let's go.

CHRISTOPHER: We might run into the boss.

WEINBERL: No, no—he's got the whole of Vienna to choose from, there's absolutely no reason why . . .

(*Distant footfalls and jingle of spurs approach. The little street echos with the sound.*)

WEINBERL: It's Nemesis!

CHRISTOPHER: Well, he's got Zangler with him!

WEINBERL: This way . . .

CHRISTOPHER: That way . . .

(*They run in opposite directions, then change their minds, then rush through the doorway into the shop. Their faces appear in the windows, one in each, watching the street cautiously as* ZANGLER *comes into view. To their consternation* ZANGLER *walks straight to the shop. The faces disappear. As* ZANGLER *turns the door handle, two voluminously swathed tartan mannequins leap into the*

36

windows, one in each. At the same moment MELCHIOR *runs in from the side while* ZANGLER *is in the doorway.*)

MELCHIOR: Sir!—Oh what luck! The Classinova person—the whosit incarnate—the Don Juan is at the Imperial Gardens Café with a nice young lady like a ladylike young niece!

ZANGLER: (*Emerging confused*) Eh, what? What? Who's this?

MELCHIOR: Herr Zangler!

ZANGLER: Your servant, sir—no, by God it's mine. What are you doing here?

MELCHIOR: I came to find you, your eminence.

ZANGLER: I told you to go straight to the restaurant.

MELCHIOR: I did but the Cassata incarnate has arrived and the tart!

ZANGLER: But that's just desserts. What about my dinner?

MELCHIOR: The dinner is all arranged, but I'm on the trail of the Casserola and you must come immediately before it gets cold.

ZANGLER: Tell them to put it in the oven. You seem to lack a sense of proportion. I am about to present myself to my fiancée in no uncertain terms, and I'm damned if I'm going to be harried and put off my stroke by the ridiculous self-importance of a jumped-up pastry-cook. Honestly, these fashionable eating houses, they think they're doing you a favour by taking your money. I told you to wait for me.

MELCHIOR: I was waiting for you, sir, and who should arrive by horsecab but Don Juan himself, reservation in the name of Sonders.

ZANGLER: There you are, you see!—I should have remained true to the Black and White Chop House.

MELCHIOR: He had a young woman with him.

ZANGLER: Of course he did—it must be three or four hours since he found himself with a vacancy.

MELCHIOR: She had a Scottish cape.

ZANGLER: Vienna has been overrun with Scottish capes, kilts, tam-o'-shanters, Royal Stuart pencil cases and highland flingery of every stripe since the town lost its head over the Verdi *Macbeth*. In my opinion it's a disgrace. Even the chocolate cake . . . Sachertartan! No, no, a Scottish cape

37

means nothing—there's even two in the window here.
(WEINBERL *and* CHRISTOPHER *hastily resume rigidity. They mustn't have a proper view of* MELCHIOR, *by the way.*)

MELCHIOR: He called her Marie.

ZANGLER: A very common name. Damn it, are you deliberately trying to nobble my—

MELCHIOR: No—

ZANGLER: No—are you deliberately trying to prick my bubble while I stand knocking at my fiancée's main entrance? I put Marie into a locked cab and promised the coachman an extra fiver if he delivered her personally into the hands of my sister-in-law, Miss Blumenblatt. What could be surer than that?

MELCHIOR: A fiver? Yes, I would say that we must be talking of two different Maries.

ZANGLER: Exactly. And what yours does is no concern of mine.

MELCHIOR: I don't think she'll do much. I had a listen and all she said was 'It isn't proper.'

ZANGLER: It's them!

MELCHIOR: No, no, a tart and ward of an entirely different clan.

ZANGLER: It's them!! Quick, fetch me a half-witted cab you hansom fool!

MELCHIOR: We're off!

ZANGLER: (*Leaving*) What a situation!

MELCHIOR: (*Following him*) Classic!

Madame Knorr's Fashion House

WEINBERL *and* CHRISTOPHER *come out of the windows into the shop.*
CHRISTOPHER *disrobes.* WEINBERL *is late and* PHILIPPINE *enters.*
WEINBERL *starts sashaying round the shop in his tartan cloak, for*
CHRISTOPHER'S *benefit.*

WEINBERL: What do you think?

CHRISTOPHER: It has a certain Scottish audacity.

WEINBERL: Ah, there you are at last. Am I addressing the arbiter of this fashion house?

PHILIPPINE: I'm sure I don't know, sir. I will fetch Madame at once. But excuse me, sir, that is a lady's cape.

38

WEINBERL: I know. I was trying it on for a lady of my size and acquaintance.

PHILLIPINE: That cape is reserved. It has a ticket on it.

WEINBERL: Yes. I know. (*Reads the ticket.*) Frau Fischer. I have come to collect it and pay for it.

CHRISTOPHER: Not exactly to pay for it.

WEINBERL: No, not exactly to pay for it, but to confirm payment. (CHRISTOPHER *has been looking out cautiously through the windows.*)

CHRISTOPHER: I think it is all clear now, Herr Fischer.

WEINBERL: Is that clear?

PHILIPPINE: I'm not sure. I'd better go and fetch Madame.

WEINBERL: Excellent idea.

CHRISTOPHER: Meanwhile we'll be off.

WEINBERL: -ally grateful if you would take care of this. (*He hands her the cape grandly.*)

PHILIPPINE: Yes, sir. Did you say Herr Fischer?

WEINBERL: Certainly. Would I pay—

CHRISTOPHER: Confirm payment.

WEINBERL: Confirm payment for somebody else's wife? (*To* CHRISTOPHER.) Why don't you see if our friend is anywhere in sight?

CHRISTOPHER: Good idea. I'll be back in a moment.

WEINBERL: Is anything the matter?

PHILIPPINE: Frau Fischer has been a widow for three years.

WEINBERL: She thinks she has, yes.

PHILIPPINE: She thinks she has? What about the funeral?

WEINBERL: It's the funeral that put the idea into her head. That she'd always be a widow. However, three days ago she did me the honour of becoming my wife.

(*To* CHRISTOPHER *who has paused in admiration on his way out.*) You will come back, won't you?

(CHRISTOPHER *goes.*)

PHILIPPINE: I'll fetch Madame immediately. She's upstairs in the workroom.

WEINBERL: Tell her there's no hurry—she's probably busy hemming and hawing.

(PHILIPPINE *goes but instantly returns.*)

39

PHILIPPINE: But, Herr Fischer, why didn't Frau Fischer change her name to yours instead of you changing your name to hers?

WEINBERL: She did. I didn't. My name, as it happens, is also Fischer. That's how we met. We were placed in alphabetical order in a fire drill at the riding academy.

PHILIPPINE: Oh, I see.

(PHILIPPINE *goes.* WEINBERL *looks cautiously into the street. While he is so engaged,* MRS FISCHER *enters the shop.* WEINBERL *bows to her and continues to look out of the window for* CHRISTOPHER's *return. After a few moments* MADAME KNORR *enters, gushing.*)

MME KNORR: There they are!—They're both here! And what a couple of naughty children you are!—Oh, my dear friend, why didn't you tell me?

MRS FISCHER: Are you feeling all right, my dear?

MME KNORR: No, I am not feeling all right. I am feeling distinctly put out. Fancy being married for three whole days without saying a word to your oldest friend and leaving your husband to break the news.

(MRS FISCHER *follows* MADAME KNORR's *gaze towards* WEINBERL.)

However, I forgive you . . . (*She walks round* WEINBERL.) And now that I see your husband I can quite understand why you kept him hidden away.

WEINBERL: What a nerve!

MRS FISCHER: My husband? (*She examines* WEINBERL *with interest.*) And he announced our marriage himself did he? (WEINBERL *flinches from her gaze, particularly when she gets out her lorgnettes to scrutinize him all the better.* MADAME KNORR *keeps gushing.*)

MME KNORR: And none too soon. Tell me, how long have you known each other?

MRS FISCHER: Not long at all.

WEINBERL: No, not long.

MME KNORR: You must have been married with your head in a whirl!

MRS FISCHER: You couldn't say I went into it with my eyes open.

40

MME KNORR: Of course you did, and I am sure you have not been disappointed.

MRS FISCHER: Surprised more than disappointed. My husband has a very individual way of dealing with the banalities of ordinary time—I expect we'll be engaged next week and exchange cards the week after.

MME KNORR: Isn't she priceless?

WEINBERL: I expect you think I'm rather presumptuous.

MRS FISCHER: No, I wouldn't say you were presumptuous. Presumption one has encountered before.

WEINBERL: Well, a little forward.

MRS FISCHER: A little? You're in danger of meeting yourself coming back.

MME KNORR: But why so sudden and secret?

MRS FISCHER: There was a reason. My dear husband will tell you.

MME KNORR: Oh do tell.

WEINBERL: My dear wife can tell you just as well as I.

MRS FISCHER: But I would like *you* to tell her.

WEINBERL: And I would like *you* to tell her—after all she's your friend.

MME KNORR: Oh dear, not quarrelling already!

MRS FISCHER: It was a whim of my dear husband's.

WEINBERL: And at the same time a whim of my dear wife's.

MME KNORR: But it is extraordinary.

WEINBERL: There is nothing extraordinary about it. When two attractive people . . .

MME KNORR: A marriage of true minds.

MRS FISCHER: Entirely.

WEINBERL: Yes, indeed. Well, I must be going.

MRS FISCHER: Going? What do you mean?

WEINBERL: I have some business to attend to.

MRS FISCHER: Aren't you going to see me try on my new Scottish cape? After all it wouldn't be fair if you didn't like it.

WEINBERL: Why?

MRS FISCHER: (*To* MADAME KNORR, *joshingly*) Why?!—isn't he the soul of generosity? If I like something, that's enough for him.

WEINBERL: Actually, I think this tartan fad is played out, you know.

MRS FISCHER: Plaid out!—such a sense of humour. I'll take it.

MME KNORR: (*To* WEINBERL) Will it be cash or account?

WEINBERL: Account, I think. Well, if that's all you wanted . . .
Delighted to have met you at last—my wife has told me so
much about you.

MRS FISCHER: Don't be so impatient, my dear.

WEINBERL: One needs a lot of patience in a marriage, I find.

MRS FISCHER: I hope I've never given you cause for complaint.

WEINBERL: Oh no.

MRS FISCHER: Have I ever contradicted you on matters large or
small?

WEINBERL: No never—much appreciated.

MRS FISCHER: Don't I do my best to enter into your ideas
against all reason?

WEINBERL: You do, you do. And since you make a point of
doing so I am sure you won't mind if I now leave you
with your friend and your Scottish cape and go about my
business.

MRS FISCHER: I would mind very much. Out of courtesy to
Madame Knorr I cannot let you forget that your only
business today is to take us out to a celebration supper.

WEINBERL: I would adore to but alas—

MRS FISCHER: Very well!—Eugenie, my dear, I'm afraid I have
to tell you—

WEINBERL: Why don't we all walk around to the Black and White
Chop House and raise a foaming tankard to our happiness.
And after that I really must dash.

MRS FISCHER: The Black and White Chop House? I'm sure it will
cause no surprise to anyone here that you would prefer to
treat us to somewhere a little better than that. We'll need a
cab.

MME KNORR: That's a wonderful idea! I do think your wife
deserves a kiss for that.

WEINBERL: Do you think so?

MME KNORR: Oh, I do!

WEINBERL: Well, I'm not going to deny anyone their due.
Permit me.

(WEINBERL *kisses* MRS FISCHER, *to her embarrassment.*)

MME KNORR: Do you call that a kiss? You don't have to stand on ceremony in front of me.

WEINBERL: Oh very well. (*He gives her a lingering kiss on the mouth.*) And in case my bride has any more good ideas I'll give her one on account.

(*He kisses her again.* CHRISTOPHER *enters the shop.*)

CHRISTOPHER: All clear.

WEINBERL: Ah, there you are. I don't think you've met my wife. This is my cousin from the country. I'm the kissing cousin, he's the country cousin. My wife—my wife's friend, Madame Knorr—my cousin—the four of us are going to have supper together at . . . (*He looks enquiringly at* MRS FISCHER.)

MRS FISCHER: The Imperial Gardens Café. Where else?

WEINBERL: The Imperial Gardens Café. Go and fetch a cab.

(*He ushers* CHRISTOPHER *out.*)

He'll be back in a few moments.

MRS FISCHER: Why don't we have a drink in the interval.

WEINBERL: Another good idea!

(*He takes her into a passionate embrace.* CHRISTOPHER *comes out of his daze. He gives a cry of delight, throws his hat in the air and runs off down the street.*)

ACT TWO

The Imperial Gardens Café
This is a conservatory ante-room. The main restaurant is off stage.
Large window in back wall, through which are visible some of the
garden, terrace, etc., and a partial view of a hansom cab, possibly
with horse attached. There is a door into this garden. There are in-
and-out swing doors to the kitchen. Stairs from the main area lead
up to a gallery at the back, from which a window looks out over the
garden where the cab is.
The place is fashionable, even pretentious; the clientele likewise. At
curtain-up we find a traffic of customers, waiters, etc. passing through
while music plays. The women's dresses suggest that the town has
gone mad for tartan. There is also a disconcerting Scottish influence
in the Vienna waltzes; bagpipes have been imported.
There are two dining tables, some chairs, a coatstand. There is a
folding screen of Chinese design.
The fashionable scene disperses and the music comes to an end.
After a pause the disembodied voices of ZANGLER *and* MELCHIOR,
who are hidden on the stage, are heard.

ZANGLER: Melchior.

MELCHIOR: Herr Zangler.

ZANGLER: What's happened to the music?

MELCHIOR: Yes, I know. It's partly the influence of German
    Pessimism, partly the decadence of an Empire that has
    outlived its purpose, and partly Scottish fortnight. I don't
    hold with it myself. Give me the evergreens every time,
    that's what I say, those golden oldies of yesteryear, the
    Blue Danube, and that other one—

ZANGLER: Melchior.

44

MELCHIOR: Yes, Herr Zangler.

ZANGLER: Shut up or I'll kill you.

MELCHIOR: Very good, Herr Zangler.

(*A jingle of spurs announces* ZANGLER's *appearance. He is wittily revealed on the stage.* MELCHIOR *remains invisible.* ZANGLER *evidently doesn't know where* MELCHIOR *is hiding.*)

ZANGLER: (*Looking round*) Melchior.

MELCHIOR: Herr Zangler.

ZANGLER: (*Looking round*) Have you seen them yet?

MELCHIOR: Not yet, Herr Zangler.

ZANGLER: Remember—absolute discretion.

MELCHIOR: Yes, Herr Zangler.

ZANGLER: (*Looking round*) Don't draw attention to yourself— blend into the background.

MELCHIOR: Very good, Herr Zangler.

ZANGLER: Where the devil are you?

MELCHIOR: Here, Herr Zangler.

ZANGLER: Ah.

(MELCHIOR *is evidently located behind the Chinese screen. He remains invisible.* ZANGLER *addresses himself to the screen.*)

Now listen. I don't want any scandal. Just keep them under observation. We may have to assume a false identity.

MELCHIOR: Classic! I'll do a waiter—they're imported here, you know.

ZANGLER: What a pretentious place. Trust my niece.

MELCHIOR: Yes, I'll do one of my foreign waiters.

ZANGLER: (*Glancing round with disgust*) La dolce vita!—pah! Cognoscenti!—pooh! (*Furiously*) Prima donna!!

MELCHIOR: Quite good—put more of a shrug into it—cognos*centi* —prima *don*na—!

(WAITER ONE *enters to move the screen to one side of the room.*)

WAITER ONE: Permettetemi signori di spostare questo paravento . . .[*Excuse me, gentlemen, may I just move this screen for you . . .*]

(*As* WAITER ONE *smartly folds the screen shut,* MELCHIOR's *voice is cut off.*)

MELCHIOR: Now that's a completely different—

(WAITER ONE *moves the screen over to the door and leaves.*

ZANGLER *follows anxiously and addresses the screen.*)

ZANGLER: Are you all right?

(ZANGLER *opens up the screen and* MELCHIOR *now makes his first appearance, limping into view, severely kinked.* ZANGLER *is relieved and at once drops the uncharacteristic solicitude.*)

Honestly, I've never known such a buffoon! I'm going to have to straighten you out when I get you home!

MELCHIOR: Thank you very much, Herr Zangler.

ZANGLER: Now go outside and have a look round.

(*Three* WAITERS *enter, one at a time, a few paces apart, from the door leading to the restaurant. They cross the stage briskly and exit through the swing door into the kitchen.*)

For all we know Sonders and Marie may have finished dinner and slipped away for the main course.

MELCHIOR: No, sir, that's their coach outside.

ZANGLER: Is it? Why didn't you tell me? Fetch the coachman in here, I want to speak to him.

MELCHIOR: At once, Herr Zangler.

(*The first* WAITER *re-enters from the kitchen carrying a veritable pagoda of crockery. He crosses briskly in the direction of the restaurant.*)

ZANGLER: And remember what I said—no scandal—complete discretion—

(*The second* WAITER *follows the first* WAITER *in a similar manner.*)

MELCHIOR: Very good, Herr Zangler—

(MELCHIOR *turns and departs efficiently through the kitchen's exit door. There is an impressive crash of falling crockery beyond the door.* MELCHIOR *re-enters through the kitchen's entrance door, knocking aside* ZANGLER *who has been drawn forward by the noise, and, apologizing to* ZANGLER *and to those he has left behind him, he hurries towards the garden door, which he opens.* MELCHIOR *shouts outside.*)

MELCHIOR: Hey you! Coachman! You're wanted in here!

COACHMAN: (*Outside, shouts*) What do you want?

MELCHIOR: In here!

ZANGLER: (*Shouting discreetly*) Discretion, damn you!

MELCHIOR: (*Whispers to* ZANGLER) Sorry.

46

(*The* COACHMAN *enters from the garden. He is a large man, immensely cloaked, wearing a tall hat; he carries a whip.*)

(*Discreetly*) Ah, coachman—my employer wishes to see you—in private—it's a matter of some delicacy—we rely on your discretion—you know what I mean?

COACHMAN: (*Roars*) Say no more, lead me to her. Where is she? (*He cracks his whip.*) If she's a goer, and has an arse a man can get a decent purchase on—

MELCHIOR: No, no!—

COACHMAN: (*Relatively quietly*) You're right!—discretion!—Tell her to meet me behind the stables. You were saying about her arse—

MELCHIOR: No . . .

ZANGLER: You there!

COACHMAN: Who's that?

MELCHIOR: My employer.

(ZANGLER *comes forward importantly and halts.*)

ZANGLER: Zangler. Import and merchandising.

COACHMAN: (*Comes forward and clicks his heels*) Bodelheimer. Transport and waiting around.

ZANGLER: Purveyor of high-class provisions, supplier of cooked meats and delicacies to the gentry.

COACHMAN: Horse manure.

ZANGLER: How dare you!

COACHMAN: I supply horse manure.

ZANGLER: Oh, I see. Well, look here, Bodelheimer, I am a man of some consequence in the Grocers' Company. You'll do what I tell you if you know what's good for your business.

COACHMAN: Horse manure. (*Astutely*) And transport.

ZANGLER: Quite. Now. You have been engaged for the evening by a man who is escorting a certain young lady in a Scottish coat—

(*The* COACHMAN *evidently has two personalities, one for sexual interests and the other for everything else. He drops the other.*)

COACHMAN: And what a corker! A pippin! She has a poise—a freshness—

ZANGLER: Quite—

47

COACHMAN: —an arse any man would give his eye teeth to sink into—

ZANGLER: That's quite enough.

COACHMAN: Happy the man who enjoys the freedom of her lacy bodice!

ZANGLER: (*Angrily*) You are addressing her guardian, sir!

COACHMAN: What are they like then?

ZANGLER: Will you be quiet!

COACHMAN: (*Quietly*) Sorry, what are they like?

ZANGLER: Now listen—

COACHMAN: Round like apples, or slightly pointy like pears?

ZANGLER: How dare you!

(*The* COACHMAN *lifts* ZANGLER *off his feet by his lapels.*)

COACHMAN: Answer me!

ZANGLER: (*Gasps*) Slightly pointy!

(*The* COACHMAN *throws him aside triumphantly.*)

COACHMAN: I knew it, by God!

(ZANGLER *reels over to* MELCHIOR.)

ZANGLER: Are you sure this is him?

COACHMAN: Conference or Williams?

ZANGLER: For God's sake, the man's obsessed!

(*But the* COACHMAN *pulls himself together suddenly and resumes his dignified personality*.)

COACHMAN: I'm sorry, your honour!—my apologies!—please disregard it. I'll be all right now.

ZANGLER: Are you quite sure?

COACHMAN: Oh yes. These attacks never last long.

ZANGLER: What sets you off?

COACHMAN: Thinking about buttocks, sir.

ZANGLER: Well, can't you keep your mind off them?

COACHMAN: I'm a coachman.

ZANGLER: Thank God we're back on the point. Now, when your passengers re-enter your coach, don't take them where they ask, but, instead, to this address which I will give you. (*He takes out a notebook and scribbles a note.*)

COACHMAN: I can't do that, they'll report me.

ZANGLER: The man is abducting my niece.

COACHMAN: I don't know about that.

ZANGLER: I do. I'll go and fetch the constable and explain to him . . . (*He jingles his purse to make the point.*) He can jump up behind and persuade them to enter the house if they give any trouble.

COACHMAN: It's out of the question.

ZANGLER: Here's half your compensation. My sister-in-law will give you the other half when you deliver the fugitives.

COACHMAN: Is she a goer then?

ZANGLER: I will follow and have the man put on a charge, and thus avoid a public scandal.

COACHMAN: Sporty type is she? Likes a good time?

ZANGLER: (*Incredulously*) Who? Miss Blumenblatt?

COACHMAN: (*Losing interest*) Oh, well, look . . .

ZANGLER: You go back to your place. As soon as they climb aboard, whip up your horses, and hand the fugitives personally to Miss Blumenblatt—

MELCHIOR: Or to her French maid.

COACHMAN: French maid?

MELCHIOR: Don't be alarmed by her manner. She's never completely dried out since falling in with a rowing eight.

COACHMAN: Where's the address?—

ZANGLER: Here. Twenty-three Carlstrasse. I will give the constable a letter.

(*The* COACHMAN *takes the note and walks smartly back to the garden and climbs up on his coach.*)

How did you know about the French maid?

MELCHIOR: You mean there is one?

ZANGLER: I'll go and fetch a constable.

MELCHIOR: What about your celebration supper with your fiancée?

ZANGLER: Sonders has ruined my plans. I'll just have some cooked goose while I'm waiting to pickle his cucumber— no—some pickled cucumber while I'm—

MELCHIOR: Got it.

(ZANGLER *leaves in the direction of the restaurant.* WAITER ONE *enters with a trolley bearing* ZANGLER's *celebration supper.*)

Ah waiter!

WAITER ONE: (*Italian accent*) Here we are—lobster—roast fowl—champagne—

MELCHIOR: Take it away—bring some beer and pickles. I want the table over here—my employer wants a clear view of the window—

WAITER ONE: What am I going to do with all this?

MELCHIOR: I am not a clairvoyant. Have you seen a young couple, the woman in a Scottish coat?

WAITER ONE: What clan?

MELCHIOR: What *clan*?

(WAITER ONE *retires with his trolley.*
From three directions the room is suddenly invaded by young couples, the women in tartan. The first couple are SONDERS *and* MARIE, *who enter from the garden and cross the room, towards the restaurant. A second couple, the* SCOTS MAN *and* WOMAN, *enter from the restaurant and go up the stairs. A third couple, the* GERMAN MAN *and* WOMAN *come down the stairs and seat themselves at the other dining table.* MELCHIOR *is completely confused by this and is uncertain which is the 'right' couple.*)

Ah!—Oh!—Wait a minute—which . . .?

(SONDERS *leads* MARIE, *in her voluminous tartan cloak and hood, through the room.*)

SONDERS: Courage, my darling—I have arranged for a friend to bring me the documents we need for an immediate marriage and tomorrow I will take you to Brussels and introduce you to my aunt as my new wife!

(SONDERS *and* MARIE *leave. The* SCOTS COUPLE, *on the gallery, move out of sight. The* GERMAN COUPLE *come down and sit at the table.* MELCHIOR, *after a couple of abortive dashes in other directions homes in on them.*)

MELCHIOR: It's them!

(*The* GERMAN COUPLE *look at him with alarm and incomprehension.* MELCHIOR *addresses them with hearty innocence.*)

Nothing! All clear! Take no notice! Carry on!

(*The* GERMAN COUPLE *nervously rise from the table and move towards the garden door.* MELCHIOR *follows them with*

elaborate courtesy.)
What weather we're having, eh? Turning out a bit dank.
Is it cold out?

GERMAN MAN: Bitte?

MELCHIOR: Is it, is it? Last night was definitely dank.
(*He opens the door for them.*) Would you say tonight was as
dank or not as dank?

GERMAN WOMAN: (*Leaving*) Danke.

MELCHIOR: (*Amazed*) Danker?

GERMAN MAN: Bitte.

MELCHIOR: (*Closing the door after them*) Please yourselves.
Sparkling couple. I don't think it's them—all they can talk
about is the weather.
Ah!
(*He notices that the* SCOTS COUPLE *are coming down the
stairs in a melodramatic way. The* WOMAN *is storming away
from her escort in some rage. The* MAN *is following her.*)

SCOTTISH MAN: Flora!

SCOTTISH WOMAN: Ye bluidy great loon, Hamish McGregor—
ye said if I came away with you ye'd take me somewhere
discreet!
(*Heading out towards the restaurant she meets* MARIE,
*similarly tartaned from head to foot, re-entering. The two
women recoil from each other in panic. The* SCOTTISH LADY
and GENTLEMAN *leave towards the restaurant, while* MARIE
enters followed by SONDERS.
SONDERS *is holding a few pieces of paper.*)

SONDERS: Here is the paper proving you are of an age to be
married without your guardian's consent.

MARIE: Oh, August, it isn't proper!

MELCHIOR: It's them!

SONDERS: I assure you it is indistinguishable from the real
thing. (*He gives her the document.*) Keep it with you at all
times.
(*He puts it into* MARIE'S *reticule. They are going out into the
garden.* MELCHIOR *whips a napkin and a menu off the table
and confronts them boldly.*)

MELCHIOR: Buona sera!—you wisha da carta?

51

SONDERS: (*Fluently*) No, grazie tante; un bel cioccolato caldo ci
aspetta alla nostra tavola in giardino, per me e per il mio
amico. [*No, thank you very much. My companion and I have
some hot chocolate waiting for us at our table in the garden.*]

MELCHIOR: Right, squire . . . Sorry . . . I thought you were
someone else.

(SONDERS *and* MARIE *leave as, to* MELCHIOR's *further
distraction,* WEINBERL *and* MRS FISCHER, *in her Scottish coat,
enter.*)

MRS FISCHER: Here we are!

WEINBERL: (*Hastily and looking nervously over his shoulder*) Look,
about us being married—

MRS FISCHER: I won't feel married until we've had our
consommé—

MELCHIOR: (*Shouts*) Oh, do what you like! What do I care if
you're married or not?

(MELCHIOR *tries to leave but meets* CHRISTOPHER *and*
MADAME KNORR, *also wearing tartan, in the doorway. To
their surprise he shrieks at them and backs out away through
the garden door.*)

MME KNORR: What a strange fellow.

MRS FISCHER: That's never happened to me before at the
Imperial Gardens Café.

WEINBERL: Yes, it's the first time for me too.

CHRISTOPHER: It happens to me every time I come.

(*They cross the stage to the further table and the coatstand,
where the women disrobe.*)

MRS FISCHER: We'll stay in here, Eugenia, do you mind? . . .
The restaurant is so crowded and frankly I had no idea
these Scottish patterns had become quite so common.

MME KNORR: It's the penalty of success, Hildegarde.

MRS FISCHER: Unfortunately the success is yours while the
penalty is mine.

(WEINBERL *and* CHRISTOPHER *are together at the table while
the women disrobe.*)

CHRISTOPHER: Well, I've reached the heights.

WEINBERL: I've got four guilders left after paying the coachman.

CHRISTOPHER: If only my mother could see me now. She never

dreamed that one day I'd be rubbing shoulders with the crème caramel!

WEINBERL: Have you got any cash?

CHRISTOPHER: People of my class don't carry cash.

WEINBERL: I only had ten guilders when we set out.

CHRISTOPHER: Ten guilders! You hoped to acquire a past for ten guilders?

WEINBERL: Well I was single then—how was I to know I'd be married for dinner?

MME KNORR: (*Approaching*) Here we are. I'm hungry.

WEINBERL: (*To* CHRISTOPHER) You're not.

CHRISTOPHER: Sit down here, my Empress.—(*To* WEINBERL.) Not what?

MME KNORR: (*To* WEINBERL) Your cousin takes great liberties considering I'm engaged to be married.

CHRISTOPHER: Be mine tonight and I will reveal my true identity and give you half my kingdom.

WEINBERL: (*To* CHRISTOPHER) Not hungry.

CHRISTOPHER: (*Snaps at him*) Not even Herzegovina, but if you don't make the best of yourself you'll end up serving in a shop.

MRS FISCHER: (*Approaching*) Has the champagne arrived yet?

WEINBERL: I don't think we should eat here. It's all together too spartan for my taste.

MME KNORR: Don't blame me—it's the penalty of—

MRS FISCHER: Spartan!—I know it's not what you're used to but Madame Knorr and I don't know any better. Where's the Mumms?—I'm dying.

CHRISTOPHER: It's probably out the back.

WEINBERL: The service here is terrible. Waiter! You see? Let's move on.

MRS FISCHER: Don't be ridiculous. Anyway you let the coachman go—I don't know why you didn't ask him to wait.

WEINBERL: I didn't care for him. He seemed a very disagreeable fellow.

MRS FISCHER: That was because of your tip.

WEINBERL: I gave him a very good tip.

CHRISTOPHER: So did I.

53

WEINBERL: Ne'er cast a clout till May is out.

CHRISTOPHER: Get into cocoa.

WEINBERL: Two very good tips.

MRS FISCHER: My husband likes to pretend he's parsimonious.

MME KNORR: You mean there's another one like him?

WEINBERL: Anyway I thought it would be nice to walk back across the park.

MRS FISCHER: Walk? Not b—

MME KNORR: There's a waiter—call him over.

WEINBERL: (*Feebly*) Waiter . . . waiter . . .

CHRISTOPER: Waiter!

WAITER TWO: Coming, sir!

WEINBERL: (*To* CHRISTOPHER) Four guilders!

CHRISTOPHER: What?

WEINBERL: (*Bowing his head*) *Four guilders* our sins as we *four guilden* that trespass against us. (*He catches* MRS FISCHER's *eye.*) Grace.

MRS FISCHER: Hildegarde. By the way, what—?

WEINBERL: Weinberl.

WAITER TWO: Are you ready to order, sir?

WEINBERL: Ah, waiter!—sit down, my dear fellow. You strike me as being a splendid chap. What will you have?

WAITER TWO: Sir?

WEINBERL: Why should we accept the places allotted to us by an economic order that sets one man above another? I've been giving this matter a great deal of thought lately, and it seems to me that, in a nutshell, the value of labour capital—

MRS FISCHER: What are you drivelling about?

WEINBERL: You may call it drivel but one day, given its chance, Weinberlism will give birth to a new order. History is waiting.

MRS FISCHER: We are *all* waiting.

WAITER TWO: I wouldn't have the special—it's herring in oatmeal.

WEINBERL: Society's accounts will be settled once and for all, and when the bill comes, waiter, I want you to think of me as a comrade.

WAITER TWO: Yes, sir. And I wouldn't have the neeps either,

if I were you.

WEINBERL: What are the neeps?

WAITER TWO: I wouldn't know, sir. That's why I wouldn't have them.

MRS FISCHER: Well, we'd like a drink to begin with.

WEINBERL: All right—bring us three beers and an extra glass.

MRS FISCHER: Such a sense of humour. He knows I never drink beer.

WEINBERL: Two beers and a glass of water.

MRS FISCHER: I must have something hot.

WEINBERL: Hot water.

MRS FISCHER: I mean something hot to eat.

WEINBERL: Two beers and a radish.

MME KNORR: You're right—he's hilarious.

MRS FISCHER: This has gone quite far enough.

WEINBERL: All right! Bring us two beers, two glasses of the house red and two sausages for the ladies.

MRS FISCHER: Two sausages?!

WEINBERL: So much the wurst for you.

(*Smartly to* CHRISTOPHER.) Get it?

CHRISTOPHER: Got it.

WEINBERL: Good—that's all we got.

(WEINBERL *hands the menu to* WAITER TWO.)

My compliments to the official receiver.

MRS FISCHER: You obviously have no idea how to entertain a lady.

CHRISTOPHER: I've got a rough idea, but let's eat first. (*He addresses* WAITER TWO *imperatively*.) You there—what's your name—we want the best dinner in the house, and we want it now!

WAITER TWO: Yes, sir! (*He clearly prefers* CHRISTOPHER's *type of customer. A thought strikes him.*) I happen to have a lobster just ready to serve.

CHRISTOPHER: Excellent.

WAITER TWO: Thermidor.

CHRISTOPHER: Excellent, Thermidor!

WAITER: And a roast fowl with all the trimmings, and for dessert you could have the plum Macduff with raspberry sauce Glencoe.

55

You get a piper with that.

CHRISTOPHER: Good. We'll drink champagne to start, champagne with the main course and with the dessert we'll have some—

WEINBERL: (*Alarmed*) Champagne?

CHRISTOPHER: Trockenbeerenauslese. You think I know nothing?

WAITER TWO: An excellent choice, sir. And if I may say so, it is a pleasure to serve a gentleman. (*He glances meaningfully at* WEINBERL *and departs.*)

WEINBERL: It's people like him who are going to put a spoke into Weinberlist Theory. (*To* CHRISTOPHER.) Nevertheless the bill will come.

CHRISTOPHER: People of my class don't pay the bill.

WEINBERL: I mean—

CHRISTOPHER: (*Very deliberately*) I know what you mean. I am not entirely stupid. Society will pay. *Our* society. Do you follow me?

WEINBERL: Not exactly . . .

CHRISTOPHER: (*Expansively*) It's a damnable thing Weinberl, but when the reckoning comes the clever people are nowhere to be found. They've gorn . . . you see . . . disappeared . . . leaving the bill to be paid by the bourgeoisie . . . the shop-keepers . . . the widows . . . and such like, get me?

WEINBERL: (*At last*) Got you!

MRS FISCHER: Oh, do stop talking politics, we came here for a celebration dinner.

(WEINBERL'*s manner has changed dramatically.*)

WEINBERL: My dear wife, why didn't you say you were hungry! We'll have a lobster *each*.

MME KNORR: Oh, it's true love.

WEINBERL: My Empress!

MRS FISCHER: (*Drily to* MADAME KNORR) Another one.

WEINBERL: I will give you half my kingdom, too!

MRS FISCHER: Hungary?

WEINBERL: Starving!

(*To* WAITER TWO *who has reappeared with the* ZANGLER *dinner trolley.*)

Ah, there you are at last—capital!—look sharp if you value your job, there's plenty of others'll do it for the money.

56

(MELCHIOR *enters from the garden with the 'Italian'* WAITER ONE. *The situation is that the* WEINBERL *party have sat themselves down at the table stage left. The* ZANGLER *table is stage right, but both tables are quite near the centre.*)

MELCHIOR: What's all this?—I've arranged for my employer to eat in here and now these people have pushed in.

CHRISTOPHER: It's a free country.

MELCHIOR: Oh, classic!

CHRISTOPHER: It wasn't meant to be original.

WAITER ONE: (*Italian accent*) There's room for everybody.

MELCHIOR: My employer wishes to eat alone.

WEINBERL: Your employer seems to be confused about the nature of this establishment. It's what we call a restaurant.

MELCHIOR: Why don't you have your dinner somewhere else?

WEINBERL: Why don't you take yourself off before you get a lobster down your britches.

(WAITER TWO *is serving up dinner for four.*)

MELCHIOR: Please! My master wishes to have a clear view of that hansom cabman while he's eating.

WEINBERL: Your master's taste in cabmen is something we prefer not to discuss.

MELCHIOR: If only this stupid place had a dividing wall.

CHRISTOPHER: Perhaps your master should arrange to be preceded everywhere by a couple of rather fetching bricklayers.

WAITER ONE: (*Italian accent*) Signor, there is a Chinese screen which we use sometimes when a customer feels the draught.

MELCHIOR: That will have to do. I'll help you with it.

MRS FISCHER: Really . . .

MME KNORR: What a nuisance!

MRS FISCHER: (*Shudders*) Chinoiserie . . . and tartan . . .

CHRISTOPHER: We can't be shown up like this in front of your wife and her friend.

(WEINBERL *and* CHRISTOPHER *get up and accost* MELCHIOR *and* WAITER ONE *who are bringing forward the screen.*)

WEINBERL: We don't intend to eat our dinner screened off from public view like a lot of—

CHRISTOPHER: Journalists—

WEINBERL: —So unless you want your Chinese screen folded

MELCHIOR: I warn you, my master will not be put out for the likes of you.

WEINBERL: You may tell your master that if he has a bone to pick with me I don't wish to see his dog. (*Something wrong with that.*) Or rather if he—

MELCHIOR: You can tell him yourself. I can hear him coming. (*The sound of spurs approaching.* WEINBERL *and* CHRISTOPHER *speak together.*)

WEINBERL:
CHRISTOPHER: } (*Levelly*) Screen.

(WEINBERL *and* CHRISTOPHER *change tack with great smoothness and take the screen in hand, moving it so that it separates the two tables.*)

WEINBERL: Let me help you—why be difficult.

CHRISTOPHER: Allow me—terrible draught in here.

MELCHIOR: Classic . . .

(ZANGLER *enters.* WEINBERL *and* CHRISTOPHER *sit down at their table visibly cowering.*)

ZANGLER: Melchior.

MELCHIOR: Your honour.

ZANGLER: Everything's arranged. The constable is poised to pursue Sonders. He's emptied my seal but his lips are pursed. No—he pursed to suppose—no—

MELCHIOR: Supper is served—

ZANGLER: No!—Oh, supper is served!

MELCHIOR: That's the boy.

(ZANGLER *sits down at his table.* WAITER ONE *sets out the beer and pickles and leaves.* WAITER TWO *wheels away the empty trolley.*)

ZANGLER: What is this screen doing here?

MELCHIOR: There's a very rough crowd at the next table—a couple of tarts and their night's work. I didn't want you to be disturbed.

ZANGLER: Good.

(*At the other table* WEINBERL *has poured the champagne. Supper commences.*)

MME KNORR: Well, life is full of surprises! I wish you all the luck in the world!

CHRISTOPHER: (*Quietly*) Thank you.

MME KNORR: I mean the newly-weds.

CHRISTOPHER: (*Quietly*) Oh yes. (*To* WEINBERL.) All the luck in the world.

WEINBERL: (*Squeakily*) Thank you.

ZANGLER: (*To* MELCHIOR) Fetch me the paper and meanwhile go and keep an eye on Sonders and Marie.

(MELCHIOR *procures, at the side of the room, a newspaper on a pole which he hands to* ZANGLER.)

They're at a table in the garden. Let me know if he gets up.

MELCHIOR: I'll throw a bucket of water over them.

ZANGLER: No—no scandal!

MRS FISCHER: . . . And not forgetting *your* wedding plans, Eugenia . . . all the luck in the world! (*She toasts* MADAME KNORR.)

MME KNORR: Thank you.

MRS FISCHER: Chink glasses.

(*They chink glasses.*)

CHRISTOPHER: (*Quietly*) All the luck in the world.

(CHRISTOPHER *chinks glasses with* MADAME KNORR.)

MME KNORR: Thank you. (*To* WEINBERL.) Thank you.

(WEINBERL *is staring into space.* CHRISTOPHER *speaks quietly to* WEINBERL.)

CHRISTOPHER: Chink glasses.

WEINBERL: (*Squeakily*) Are they? They must go with the screen.

MRS FISCHER: Why are you speaking like that?

WEINBERL: (*Squeaks*) Like what?

MRS FISCHER: You're speaking in a peculiar way.

WEINBERL: (*To* CHRISTOPHER) Am I?

CHRISTOPHER: (*Quietly*) Not that I noticed.

MME KNORR: (*To* CHRISTOPHER) What's happened to your voice?

CHRISTOPHER: (*Quietly*) Nothing—there's no need to shout.

MME KNORR: I'm not shouting, I'm speaking normally.

WEINBERL: (*Squeaks*) Not so loud.

MRS FISCHER: And why aren't you eating?—lost your appetite?

CHRISTOPHER: (*Quietly to* WEINBERL) Chicken?

WEINBERL: (*Squeaks*) Wouldn't you be?

MME KNORR: I'd like some chicken. And some more champagne.
I can feel it working already.

CHRISTOPHER: (*Quietly*) Breast or leg?

MME KNORR: All over.

CHRISTOPHER: (*Quietly to* WEINBERL) Breast or leg?

WEINBERL: (*Squeaks*) I'll take wing—have you got it?

CHRISTOPHER: (*Quietly*) Got it. (*To* MADAME KNORR.) The
bottle's empty. I'll get a waiter.

(CHRISTOPHER *gets up and moves to the coatstand where,*
unnoticed by the women, he puts on MRS FISCHER's *full-length*
tartan coat and puts the hood over his head.)

WEINBERL: (*Squeaks*) I'll get one too.

MRS FISCHER: We don't need two waiters.

WEINBERL: (*Squeaks*) All right, I'll help him get the first one.

MRS FISCHER: Don't be silly—

MME KNORR: Oh, look—I've got the wish-bone!

WEINBERL: Have you?

MME KNORR: Come on, Hildegarde—

(MADAME KNORR *and* MRS FISCHER *pull the wish-bone.*)

Ah, well done! You've got the main part.

WEINBERL: (*Squeaks to* MADAME KNORR) That means it's your
wish.

MME KNORR: No—it's your wife's wish.

WEINBERL: (*Squeaks*) That's not how we play it.

MRS FISCHER: I'm beginning to regret that I ever married you.

WEINBERL: You'd better both have a wish.

MME KNORR: Oh—all right—

WEINBERL: Close your eyes and don't tell me what you wish.

(MADAME KNORR *and* MRS FISCHER *close their eyes.* CHRISTOPHER
has crept along the back wall into ZANGLER's *area and leaves*
through the garden door. ZANGLER *is distracted by his news-*
paper.)

ZANGLER: (*Shakes his head sadly*) Knocked out in the first round
of the sheep-dog trials . . . (*Then puzzled.*) What paper is
this?

(*Meanwhile* WEINBERL *has crept away up the stairs and is*
leaving by the gallery window in order to drop into the cab.
MRS FISCHER *opens her eyes and finds him gone.*)

MRS FISCHER: My God, it works.

(ZANGLER *sees* CHRISTOPHER *enter the cab and* WEINBERL *also.* ZANGLER *jumps up in great excitement as* MELCHIOR *rushes in from the garden.*)

MELCHIOR: Herr Zangler!—I don't understand—I just saw—

ZANGLER: We've got them! And, look, the constable has jumped up behind.

(SONDERS *enters from the garden in a huff, followed by* MARIE.)

SONDERS: Where is the proprietor of this madhouse? Two people have just leapt into my cab and—(*He sees* ZANGLER.)

ZANGLER: Sonders!

MARIE: Uncle!

(ZANGLER *jumps out of his chair, knocking over the screen.* MADAME KNORR *and* MRS FISCHER *leap up in horror and confusion.*)

MME KNORR: Zangler!

ZANGLER: My fiancée.

(*Amid squeals and protestations, the pudding enters accompanied by the* PIPER.

With ZANGLER *and the women in a general state of dismay and distress,* MELCHIOR *restores the screen to its vertical position, struggling with it, and ending up concealed behind it with everybody else.*

The PIPER, *with a long vertical tartan sash falling from his shoulder, the tartan bagpipe under his arm, and tartan ribbons fluttering from the stem over his shoulder, the pipes bawling, moves from stage right, disappears behind the screen and re-emerges, no longer in the restaurant, in the form of the* CONSTABLE, *carrying the bawling* CHRISTOPHER *over his shoulder.*)

CONSTABLE: Not so much noise or I'll have you for breaking the peace.

(*The* COACHMAN *is now following him at a few paces' distance, frogmarching a protesting* WEINBERL.)

WEINBERL: What's going on?! Where are we going?

COACHMAN: Twenty-three Carlstrasse.

CONSTABLE: Nearly there.

(*The two struggling couples pass out of sight.*)

Living room, MISS BLUMENBLATT's *flat*
Double entrance doors, interior door, window to dark exterior, the
bottom of a staircase, and another exit route which could be a chimney.
Geraniums in pots. Candlesticks.

MISS BLUMENBLATT *is sitting reading the newspaper aloud to* LISETTE,
the French maid.

MISS BLUMENBLATT: '. . . In deploring these scenes of un-
Austrian excess, we do not make the error of confusing
café society with society in general. Yet the example of the
Roman Empire lies ever before us. When those who
presume to set standards are seen to have abandoned decent
Aryan values for the degenerate postures of an alien culture,
we say enough is enough. We have nothing against the
Celtic race as such. We are assured that the Celts have a
long and obscure history, and have made their contribution,
such as it is, to science and the arts. But their ways are not
our ways, and we cannot but condemn this infatuation with
the barbarian baroque universe of Sir Walter Scotch and
his ilk. It is a moral issue . . .'
That's all very well, but it doesn't stop them advertising
Hunting-Stuart underdrawers in the same paper. Hardly
comme il faut.

LISETTE: Oui, Madame, 'ardly like he must. But 'ow late it is
for our guest not arriving.

MISS BLUMENBLATT: I can't think what has happened. My
brother-in-law's letter definitely said that he was sending
Marie to my safe keeping today. I was looking forward to
seeing the dear child again after these ten years. She will
find me more sympathique than Zangler has bargained
for. Her fate is just like my own. I too know what it is to
have loved and to have been separated from the man who
stole my heart . . .

LISETTE: Oh, Madame, 'ow I long for a man to steal mine!
'Ow will I know when it 'appens?

MISS BLUMENBLATT: You will know, never fear. With me it was
on a horse-tram in the Bahnhofstrasse . . . The chestnut
trees were in bloom . . . He sat down opposite me. Our
eyes met. I smiled.

LISETTE: What 'appened to 'im, Madame?

MISS BLUMENBLATT: He jumped off between stops and I never
saw him again. But it was still love, and it was still
separation. I'll never forget the pain as he rolled out of my
sight for ever!

(*Approaching sound of bawling.*)

Is that those people next door playing the bagpipes again?

LISETTE: I think it is a commotion outside. I will go to see.

(LISETTE *goes out through the double doors, leaving them
open, opens an unseen door. She screams. The front door
slams and* LISTETTE *is borne back into the room over the
shoulder of the* COACHMAN. LISETTE's *skirts have ridden up to
reveal her Hunting-Stuart underdrawers.* MISS BLUMENBLATT
rises to her feet, swaying.)

MISS BLUMENBLATT: Lisette!—déshabillé!—

COACHMAN: Hang about—which one of you is the French bit?

(MISS BLUMENBLATT *swoons.*)

Oh dear—

(*He looks round and puts* LISETTE *down on her feet.*)

A thousand apologies!

(*He turns solicitously towards* MISS BLUMENBLATT, *but
LISETTE swoons where he stood her and he turns around just
in time to catch her and lower her into a chair, as there is a
knocking and ringing at the door.*)

Sorry! (*Shouts*) Just a minute!

(*In a dither, the* COACHMAN *hesitates between the two
insensible women. He tears a strip of* MISS BLUMENBLATT's
*newspaper, ignites it in the candle flame, blows out the flaming
paper and wafts the smoulding end under* LISETTE's *nose.*)

Please disregard . . . I'll be all right now . . .

(*The knocking and ringing is renewed.*)

(*Desperately*) Just a minute!!

(LISETTE *starts to revive.*)

It's these cold nights—the steam rising off their sleek
rippling haunches—

(*He sees that* LISETTE *has come round and turns his attention
to* MISS BLUMENBLATT *but* LISETTE *stops him.*)

LISETTE: Wait! (*She leaps up and kisses him firmly on the mouth.*)

At last!

COACHMAN: (*Highly gratified*) Are you a goer?

LISETTE: I am a goer! You have horses?

COACHMAN: I have the finest pair of chestnuts of any coachman in the city.

(LISETTE *half swoons in his arms.*)

(*Bewildered*) What did I say?

LISETTE: (*Reviving*) My window will be open. Get up with me on your high horse.

(LISETTE *rushes to the front door to answer the knocking. The* COACHMAN *returns to* MISS BLUMENBLATT *who is just starting to come round.*)

MISS BLUMENBLATT: Oh!—cauchemar!

COACHMAN: (*Kindly*) Coach-man . . .

(*The* CONSTABLE *enters, frogmarching* WEINBERL *and* CHRISTOPHER, *who is still in travesty.* LISETTE *follows and closes the double doors.*)

CONSTABLE: In you go and no arguments.

WEINBERL: Someone is going to pay for this.

CONSTABLE: What makes you think they haven't?

CHRISTOPHER: I'm not the woman you think I am. I'm not even the woman you *think* is the woman you think I am.

MISS BLUMENBLATT: (*Rising to her feet*) Enough!—is enough! To what am I owed this scene of un-Austrian excess? (*To* LISETTE.) And don't think I didn't notice your McIntosh bloomers or whatever they were!

COACHMAN: Mackintosh bloomers!—she's the woman of my dreams.

LISETTE: (*Defensively*) They do keep out the mist.

MISS BLUMENBLATT: Who are all these people? What are they doing here?

CONSTABLE: My instructions are that this couple are to remain here until the arrival of your brother-in-law.

MISS BLUMENBLATT: What? Surely this can't be the young woman?

WEINBERL: Of course she isn't—

CHRISTOPHER: And I can prove it.

WEINBERL: —if she has to. (*To* CHRISTOPHER.) At the same time

64

we don't want to be taken for someone who leaves society to pay his bills.

CONSTABLE: It's all explained in the letter.

MISS BLUMENBLATT: Let me have it.

(CONSTABLE *hands her* ZANGLER's *letter.*)

WEINBERL: Thank heavens! Now you can see that my friend and I are the innocent victims of a police force the like of which would explode the credibility of a comic opera.

CONSTABLE: I have a duty to keep the peace.

WEINBERL: To the devil with your duty!

CHRISTOPHER: I don't wish to be offensive, constable, but it seems to me that you're as full of wind as a newt.

WEINBERL: And your peace to boot!

CHRISTOPHER: He certainly is!

MISS BLUMENBLATT: (*Folding up the letter*) Ah—now I understand.

WEINBERL: Thank goodness—where's my hat?

MISS BLUMENBLATT: Lisette . . . you know where we keep the tin of broken biscuits. Take the coachman into the kitchen and give him one.

LISETTE: Oui, Madame. Walk zis way.

COACHMAN: (*Following* LISETTE *out, mutters*) Mackintosh bloomers . . .

MISS BLUMENBLATT: And you, constable, will you have a piece of oval Marie?

CONSTABLE: Not while I'm on duty. I'll station myself on the front steps and wait for your brother-in-law. (*He lets himself out through the double doors.*)

WEINBERL: We must be going too—we have a long way to get home.

CHRISTOPHER: Yes, and somebody really ought to give us our fare for our trouble.

MISS BLUMENBLATT: (*Barring their way*) Stop! You are not leaving here.

WEINBERL: What!

CHRISTOPHER: It wasn't our fault. Don't blame us.

(MISS BLUMENBLATT *takes him into an embrace.*)

MISS BLUMENBLATT: My dear child—of course I don't blame

you! Your fate is exactly like my own. It happened to me on a horse-tram in the Bahnhofstrasse!

WEINBERL: You mean, the minute you got on it took off like a rocket—?

MISS BLUMENBLATT: I mean *love*! Oh, you have behaved recklessly but who can gainsay the power of love? And you, sir, you have much to answer for but do not give up hope. I am not the woman you think I am.

CHRISTOPHER: What? You don't mean—

WEINBERL: Of course she doesn't—Madame, would you mind telling us exactly what is in that letter?

MISS BLUMENBLATT: Only what you would expect a possessive guardian to write when his virgin niece has been abducted by a notorious Don Juan.

WEINBERL: He's as wrong about me as he is about her.

CHRISTOPHER: Wronger if anything.

MISS BLUMENBLATT: Of course he is. Have no fear. I will see you married in the morning.

WEINBERL: (*Without thinking*) Thank you. No—I think we ought to wait—she's so young, and I'd like to sleep on it, elsewhere—

(*The doorbell is heard.*)

MISS BLUMENBLATT: (*Shouts*) Lisette!

(*The kitchen door opens smartly and* LISETTE *appears, breathing heavily, her maid's cap back to front, the tartan ribbons falling over her face. She marches to the door.*)
Did he take the biscuit?

LISETTE: He is taking it now, Madame. (*She opens the double doors and goes to the unseen front door.*)

MISS BLUMENBLATT: (*To* CHRISTOPHER) This may be your uncle.

CHRISTOPHER: None too soon.

WEINBERL: This'll clear things up.

(LISETTE *appears with* MELCHIOR.)
. . . or not.

LISETTE: This man insists on being admitted. (*She continues towards the kitchen and leaves without ceremony.*)

MELCHIOR: Fraulein Blumenblatt!

MISS BLUMENBLATT: Well, sir?

(WEINBERL *and* CHRISTOPHER *are naturally surprised and dismayed*.)

CHRISTOPHER: That's—

WEINBERL: Zangler's servant!

MELCHIOR: My employer has sent me ahead to explain to you that this young couple who got into the coach are not actually the young couple—(*He notices* WEINBERL.)

MELCHIOR: It's you!

MISS BLUMENBLATT: Of course it's them! Do you know this man, Herr Sonders?

(WEINBERL *looks around in surprise and then realizes that he is being addressed*.)

WEINBERL: Sonders?

CHRISTOPHER: Marie's lover! She must think I'm—

MISS BLUMENBLATT: What's the matter, Marie?

CHRISTOPHER: (*Panicking faintly*) Oh, I've got it!

WEINBERL: (*Terrified*) I think I gave it to you.

MELCHIOR: Shame on you, sir!

MISS BLUMENBLATT: Don't be impertinent.

MELCHIOR: But this man is—

MISS BLUMENBLATT: I know all about that—

MELCHIOR: My employer was obliged to pay this man's bill.

MISS BLUMENBLATT: What bill?

MELCHIOR: To save two ladies from being turned over to the police.

MISS BLUMENBLATT: What ladies?

MELCHIOR: And now he's got another one. (*To* CHRISTOPHER.) Don't have dinner with him, miss!—he will pudding you before the dessert—no—he'll desert you before—

MISS BLUMENBLATT: What is all this nonsense? Who sent you?

MELCHIOR: Your brother-in-law, Herr Zangler. He mistook this man for Sonders, and this lady for his niece—

WEINBERL: Exactly! So he wants you to let us go before he gets here—

(*The doorbell sounds again*.)

MISS BLUMENBLATT: (*Shouts*) Lisette!

WEINBERL: Is there a back door?

(*The kitchen door bursts open and* LISETTE *stands hatless, swaying. She pulls herself together and marches out towards the front door.*

WEINBERL *turns his attention to the window and opens it.*

MISS BLUMENBLATT *addresses* MELCHIOR, *holding* ZANGLER'S *letter.*)

MISS BLUMENBLATT: But that's the exact opposite of what it says in this letter. You're obviously not to be trusted.

(LISETTE *reappears in the double doors.*)

LISETTE: Herr Weinberl is here.

(WEINBERL *has one leg over the windowsill. He pauses.*)

WEINBERL: Who?

LISETTE: Herr Weinberl. He says he is Herr Zangler's chief sales assistant.

(WEINBERL *puts his leg back into the room.*)

MISS BLUMENBLATT: I've heard Zangler speak of him. What does he want?

LISETTE: He says, has Miss Marie arrived yet because Herr Zangler has changed his mind and wants Herr Weinberl to take the young lady away.

MISS BLUMENBLATT: We'll see about that. Send him in.

(LISETTE *goes.*)

Don't concern yourself. You haven't a care in the world.

(LISETTE *reappears with* SONDERS.)

LISETTE: Herr Weinberl.

(LISETTE *makes a dignified but determined exit to the kitchen.* SONDERS *bows.*)

SONDERS: Madam, my apologies for calling so late. Weinberl.

MISS BLUMENBLATT: I'm delighted to make your acquaintance. Let me introduce you to Herr Sonders.

(WEINBERL *and* SONDERS *scrutinize each other suspiciously.*)

Herr Sonders . . . Herr Weinberl.

Herr Weinberl . . . Herr Sonders.

But perhaps you two already know each other.

WEINBERL: (*Stiffly*) I don't believe I've had the honour.

SONDERS: No, I don't believe so.

(SONDERS *is very aware of* CHRISTOPHER *who is hiding his face in his hood.*)

68

I know Marie, of course . . .

(SONDERS *reaches for* CHRISTOPHER's *hand and kisses it.*
MELCHIOR *is puzzled and mutters to himself.*)

MELCHIOR: Sonders—Weinberl—Weinberl—Sonders—Wait a
minute . . . that's surely . . .

SONDERS: Marie and I must leave immediately. This way, my
dear, your uncle is waiting for us—

MISS BLUMENBLATT: Just one moment, Herr Weinberl. Kindly
desist from ordering people in and out of my house as if it
were a blazing cuckoo-clock. Marie happens to be in love
with Herr Sonders.

SONDERS: Well, yes and no—

MELCHIOR: Excuse me . . .

MISS BLUMENBLATT: (*Shouts*) Yes and no! The moment they met
she was absolutely bowled over. It is something I can
understand because her fate is precisely my own, except
that in my case it was a horse-tram in the Bahnhofstrasse.

SONDERS: You were run over by a tram?

MELCHIOR: Madam . . .

MISS BLUMENBLATT: Furthermore one only has to look at Herr
Sonders to see that he is no Don Juan. Look into his
eyes. I have seen more treachery in a cocker
spaniel.

(*She takes* WEINBERL *by the arm and turns aside to confer
with him.*)

This is what we must do. I will send Zangler a message
with this Weinberl to come here and . . .

(SONDERS *is making sidelong attempts to capture* CHRISTOPHER's
attention. CHRISTOPHER *is cowering from the possibility.*)

SONDERS: Marie . . . Marie . . . Who is this impostor? How . . .?

(*Meanwhile* MELCHIOR *is scrutinizing* SONDERS *from closer
range.* MELCHIOR *grabs him.*)

MELCHIOR: This is the real one!

SONDERS: How dare you!

MISS BLUMENBLATT: What . . .?

MELCHIOR: He is the impostor!

SONDERS: What does this man want? Who are you?

MISS BLUMENBLATT: You mean you don't know him? And he's

69

been putting himself about as Zangler's servant! I knew he wasn't to be trusted! (*Shouts*) Lisette!

(*The kitchen door crashes open.* LISETTE *sways in the doorway, glazed, discreetly disarrayed, utterly changed.*)

Fetch the constable in here.

(LISETTE *passes through on the errand like a practised drunk.*)

MELCHIOR: The constable? I hope, madam, you're not thinking of—

MISS BLUMENBLATT: I'm not thinking of anything. I am having you arrested.

MELCHIOR: (*Aghast*) Me?

MISS BLUMENBLATT: For false impersonation.

MELCHIOR: This place is teeming with frauds! I am about the only person here who isn't pretending to be somebody else!

(*The* CONSTABLE *enters.* LISETTE *remains outside.*)

CONSTABLE: Who is it you want helping with enquiries?

MISS BLUMENBLATT: This man here.

MELCHIOR: Leave me alone.

(*The* CONSTABLE *grapples with him.*)

I'll have the law on you!

CONSTABLE: I don't think you've thought that through.

SONDERS: Get rid of him.

WEINBERL: Yes, the man's a menace.

(LISETTE *now appears in the doorway.*)

LISETTE: Herr Zangler is here. With his fiancée and Madame Fischer and his niece.

(*In the moment between her announcement and* ZANGLER's *entry,* SONDERS, WEINBERL *and* CHRISTOPHER *leave the room by different routes but with identical timing.* WEINBERL *leaves by the window.* CHRISTOPHER *goes up the stairs.* SONDERS *leaves by the chimney, if possible.*

ZANGLER *comes in with* MADAME KNORR *and* MRS FISCHER *on his arm and* MARIE *following.*

The CONSTABLE *pauses but still keeps hold of* MELCHIOR.

LISETTE, *without pause, goes straight back to the kitchen.*)

ZANGLER: Here we are, better late than never! What a night it's been!

MELCHIOR: Oh, thank goodness—

70

ZANGLER: First things first. Let me introduce my fiancée and my fiancée's friend, Madame Fischer—Fräulein Blumenblatt . . .

MISS BLUMENBLATT: Enchantée.

ZANGLER: And this is my ward, Marie.

MISS BLUMENBLATT: Are you sure?

ZANGLER: The wedding is tomorrow.

MISS BLUMENBLATT: (*Looking round and noticing their absence*) What happened to Herr Sonders and . . .?

ZANGLER: Not *her* wedding—my wedding.

MISS BLUMENBLATT: Such haste?

ZANGLER: I'm not letting Madame Knorr out of my sight until we're married. I have my reasons.

MISS BLUMENBLATT: (*Excitedly*) Madame Knorr? Not the celebrated Madame Knorr they say gets her models straight from Paris?

ZANGLER: Apparently not. Why has the constable got my Melchior by the geraniums?

MISS BLUMENBLATT: You mean he's really—?

MELCHIOR: Oh, tell her who I am!

ZANGLER: He's my servant, of course.

(*The* CONSTABLE *releases* MELCHIOR.)

MELCHIOR: And do you have a salesman called Weinberl?

ZANGLER: I have.

MELCHIOR: Where is he now?

ZANGLER: At home fast asleep above the shop.

MELCHIOR: I rest my case.

MRS FISCHER: Weinberl! Wasn't that the name of—?

MME KNORR: It was! The one with the cousin who stole your coat!

MISS BLUMENBLATT: Not a tartan coat with a hood just like Marie's?

MRS FISCHER: Yes, I'm afraid it was.

ZANGLER: Surely it can't have been Weinberl.

MISS BLUMENBLATT: They were here!

MELCHIOR: I told you it wasn't Sonders.

MRS FISCHER: It was my so-called husband.

ZANGLER: Well, was he so-called or wasn't he? Where is he?

MISS BLUMENBLATT: He was here just now. And the window is open.

71

(ZANGLER *rushes to and through the window*.)

ZANGLER: My God, I was just about to make him my partner!
If I find he's been on the razzle—
(MELCHIOR *is helping* ZANGLER *out through the window, and he
follows*.)

MELCHIOR: (*Disappearing*) Classic!
(*Sounds of* ZANGLER *and* MELCHIOR *rushing round the
garden.* MADAME KNORR *watches from the window*.)

MME KNORR: (*Fondly*) Isn't he masterful? Did you notice the
spurs?

MRS FISCHER: I think I prefer him to your first husband,
Eugenia.

MME KNORR: Oh yes, *he* had two left feet, poor Alfred . . .

MISS BLUMENBLATT: What happened to him?

MME KNORR: He got knocked down by a horse-tram in the
Bahnhofstrasse.

MISS BLUMENBLATT'*s garden*
*A high wall running across the stage with a door set into it. The side
of* MISS BLUMENBLATT'*s house. Door into house from garden. Upper
bedroom window.*

ZANGLER *and* MELCHIOR *are, as it were, beating the bushes.*

ZANGLER: The garden is completely walled in and the gate is
locked, but there's no sign of them. What's happened to
the coachman?

MELCHIOR: He's very thick with the parlourmaid, apparently.

ZANGLER: Well, he's supposed to remain outside.

MELCHIOR: He didn't want to frighten the horses.

ZANGLER: Tell him to bring his coach round to the gate. If we
set off now we'll be home by first light. Weinberl won't be
expecting me back so early, I'll catch him on the hop. If
it's the same Weinberl, he's finished in high-class
groceries—I'll see to that.
(LISETTE *enters the garden from the house in great
excitement. Light spills from the open door*.)

LISETTE: Monsieur! One of the persons is fled to my room.

ZANGLER: Lock the door on him!

LISETTE: The person, he has locked it.

ZANGLER: Break it down!

LISETTE: I have another key.

(LISETTE, ZANGLER *and* MELCHIOR *pile back into the house, closing the door and leaving the garden dark again.* WEINBERL *comes out of hiding.* Moonlight)

WEINBERL: (*Whispering loudly*) Christopher!
(*He looks round vainly.* CHRISTOPHER *is at the upstairs window however.*)

CHRISTOPHER: (*Whispering loudly*) Herr Weinberl!

WEINBERL: Is that you?

CHRISTOPHER: Yes!

WEINBERL: Can you get down?

CHRISTOPHER: No. Can you get over the wall?

WEINBERL: No. We're done for.

CHRISTOPHER: I can hear somebody outside my door.

WEINBERL: I'm sorry, Christopher.

CHRISTOPHER: It wasn't your fault, Mr Weinberl. Thank you for everything. It was a wonderful razzle.

WEINBERL: Yes. Not bad, really. To hell with them.

CHRISTOPHER: (*Urgently*) There's somebody coming behind you!
(WEINBERL *goes back into hiding.* SONDERS *approaches cautiously with a ladder.* SONDERS, *looking around in the dark.*)

SONDERS: (*Whispers*) Marie . . .

CHRISTOPHER: August! . . .
(SONDERS *looks up and sees him.*)

SONDERS: Marie! Courage, my darling! I have a ladder!

CHRISTOPHER: (*Unwisely*) First class!

SONDERS: Is that really you?

CHRISTOPHER: (*Changing tack*) Oh, August, it isn't proper!

SONDERS: It's you! Be brave, my little dove, trust me—(*He puts the ladder up against the window.*)

CHRISTOPHER: I will, I will! (*He comes down the ladder.*)

SONDERS: Have you got the documents?
(CHRISTOPHER *gasps in dismay.*)
Where are they?

73

(CHRISTOPHER *points dramatically upwards.*)
I'll have to go and get them.
(SONDERS *goes up the ladder. As he does so there is the clatter of hooves, and the* COACHMAN's *hat and head and shoulders are seen travelling aloft beyond the wall. The coach comes to a halt, unseen, so that it would be opposite the doorway in the wall.*
At the same time, SONDERS *climbs into the bedroom . . . which is flooded with light as an interior door opens, bringing* LISETTE *into the room, carrying a lamp.*
WEINBERL *has emerged out of hiding, and he and* CHRISTOPHER *have just grasped the ladder with a view to removing it from the window. But there is a commotion between* LISETTE *and* SONDERS.)
COACHMAN: Lisette!
(*The* COACHMAN *climbs easily from the unseen coach on to the wall.* WEINBERL *and* CHRISTOPHER *jump back into the darkness. The* COACHMAN *lowers himself down the inside of the wall and rushes up the ladder into* LISTETTE's *bedroom. As he breasts the sill he takes off his hat and throws it into the room at* SONDERS. *He disappears into the room, the lamp is extinguished.*
At the same time the door from the house is flung open. It releases, in a high state of excitement, ZANGLER, MELCHIOR, MADAME KNORR, MRS FISCHER, MARIE *and* MISS BLUMENBLATT.)
ZANGLER: There's a ladder! They've got away! Unlock the gate!
(MISS BLUMENBLATT *runs forward with a large key and unlocks the gate in the wall.*)
Where's the coachman?
(*From the now darkened bedroom,* SONDERS, *wearing the* COACHMAN's *hat and cloak, descends by the ladder.*
Everybody else, except MISS BLUMENBLATT, *who is holding the gate open, is passing through the wall and straight into the interior of the coach outside the gate.* MARIE *is last in the queue.* SONDERS *removes the ladder from the window and places it against the wall.*)
SONDERS: (*To* MARIE) Courage, my darling!
(MARIE *gasps and passes through into the coach.*

74

SONDERS *goes up the ladder and takes the* COACHMAN's *seat. Everybody is now inside the coach.*
WEINBERL *and* CHRISTOPHER *come out of the dark, hurriedly climb the ladder and get on to the roof of the coach just as it starts to move.*
LISETTE *comes to the window.*)
LISETTE: (*To* MISS BLUMENBLATT) Madame! The coach is taking away the sweetheart of Miss Marie!
MISS BLUMENBLATT: My own case exactly. Except, of course, that it was a horse-tram in the Bahnhofstrasse.

ZANGLER's *shop*
The coach is now seen through the panes of ZANGLER's *shop window. The occupants are all unpacking themselves from the interior.*
SONDERS *gets down from the coach.* WEINBERL *and* CHRISTOPHER *have travelled here on the roof of the coach.*
ZANGLER, MADAME KNORR, MRS FISCHER, MARIE *and* MELCHIOR *disappear noisily from view and enter the* ZANGLER *premises off stage. None of this is especially explicit. The stage is mainly occupied, of course, by the empty interior of the shop. It is early morning and the shop is not open yet.*
WEINBERL *and* CHRISTOPHER *try the shop door from the outside, unsuccessfully. There is a desperation about them and they disappear from view. Meanwhile,* ZANGLER *has been heard from within shouting for* WEINBERL.
ZANGLER: (*Off stage*) They're not upstairs— they're not downstairs—if they're not in the shop we've got them!
(*The trap door in the floor opens and* CHRISTOPHER *emerges. He drops the trap door as* ZANGLER *hurries into the shop.* ZANGLER *is somewhat taken aback by seeing* CHRISTOPHER.)
Ah—it's you.
CHRISTOPHER: Good morning, Herr Zangler. (*He goes to the street door and starts unbolting it.*) Just opening up, Herr Zangler!
ZANGLER: Where's Weinberl?
CHRISTOPHER: He's here, Herr Zangler.
ZANGLER: Where?

CHRISTOPHER: Where?

ZANGLER: Yes, where?

CHRISTOPHER: You mean, where is he now, Herr Zangler?

ZANGLER: (*Impatiently*) Yes, yes—

CHRISTOPHER: Herr Weinberl—?

ZANGLER: *Yes!*—Where is Herr Weinberl now, you numskull!
(WEINBERL *plummets out of the chute and arrives behind the
counter in a serving position.*)

WEINBERL: Good morning, Herr Zangler. How was the parade?

ZANGLER: Weinberl . . . My dear fellow . . . I thought . . .
(*There is a general entry now. Firstly,* SONDERS *enters from
the street door which has just been opened by* CHRISTOPHER.
MARIE *enters from the house, followed by* MADAME KNORR,
MRS FISCHER *and* MELCHIOR.)
(*To* MARIE.) What do you want? (*Sees* SONDERS.) Oh—the
coachman—pay him from the till—
(MARIE *goes to the till and* SONDERS *goes to the counter.*
ZANGLER's *attention turns to* MADAME KNORR *and* MRS
FISCHER. MRS FISCHER *reacts to* WEINBERL's *presence behind
the counter and she approaches him so that only the counter is
between them.*
Meanwhile MADAME KNORR *is taking in the presence of*
CHRISTOPHER.)
May I present my faithful partner, Herr Weinberl. We owe
him an apology, I feel . . . and my chief sales assistant,
Christopher . . . my fiancée . . . Madame Knorr . . .

CHRISTOPHER: Enchanted. Haven't we met before?

ZANGLER: What?

MME KNORR: No!

CHRISTOPHER: No, I thought not.

ZANGLER: And Madame Fischer . . . you don't know Herr
Weinberl.

MRS FISCHER: On the contrary—I am well acquainted with Herr
Weinberl.

ZANGLER: You are?

WEINBERL: You're not, are you? (WEINBERL *seems about to
swoon. He grasps the pull-handle of the cash-canister above
him.*)

76

MRS FISCHER: How can you say that after writing me all those romantic letters?—Scaramouche! (*She picks up for evidence the letter which* WEINBERL *left lying on the counter in Act One.*)

WEINBERL: Elegant And Under Forty!

ZANGLER: Well!

(WEINBERL *pulls the handle and releases cash-canister which travels along the wire knocking off* SONDERS's *hat.* SONDERS *is recognized as himself by all.*)

Sonders!

SONDERS: Herr Zangler!

ZANGLER: I'll kill him!

MARIE: Oh, Uncle!

(*The* BELGIAN FOREIGNER *enters from the street, rather dramatically.*)

FOREIGNER: Herr Sonders!

(*Everybody stops and gives him their attention.*)

SONDERS: Go away—for God's sake are you still dogging me for a miserable unpaid hat-bill?

(*The* FOREIGNER *has evidently gone to some trouble overnight to master the necessary phrases he requires. He has written some of them down on white postcards from which he now reads in a declamatory manner.*)

FOREIGNER: Herr Sonders! I am coming from Brussels. I am coming from the lawyer of your relatively departed ant.

SONDERS: What?

FOREIGNER: Alas, your ant is mortified!

SONDERS: Mortified?

FOREIGNER: As a door nail.

SONDERS: My aunt! How dreadful! You mean my dear auntie in Brussels has unfortunately passed away?

FOREIGNER: (*Pointing to* SONDERS) This man is too rich!

MARIE: Oh, oh darling, does this mean . . .?

SONDERS: (*To* ZANGLER.) Sir . . .

ZANGLER: Ah—yes, indeed—Julie, isn't it?

SONDERS: August.

ZANGLER: August, of course . . . my dears . . . (*To* FOREIGNER.) How much exactly . . .? Well, never mind for now—I

77

think we all deserve a champagne breakfast . . . we have
two or three happy couples to toast, I believe . . .

(ZANGLER *starts shepherding everybody out of the shop. The*
FOREIGNER *goes too.* MELCHIOR *hangs back.*)

SONDERS: Marie!

(*He takes* MARIE's *arm and they leave.*)

ZANGLER: Eugenia!

(*He takes* MADAME KNORR's *arm and they leave.*
WEINBERL *joins the recessional, offering his arm to* MRS
FISCHER.)

WEINBERL: Hildergarde . . .

(MRS FISCHER *slaps his face and departs alone.*
This leaves WEINBERL, CHRISTOPHER *and* MELCHIOR.)

ZANGLER: (*Outside*) Melchior!

(WEINBERL *and* CHRISTOPHER *simultaneously realize that they*
could still be undone.)

WEINBERL: Melchior!

(*But* MELCHIOR *spreads his palms in reassurance and*
admiration.)

MELCHIOR: Classic! Coming, Herr Zangler!

(MELCHIOR *goes out.*
WEINBERL *and* CHRISTOPHER *go to their places behind the*
counter. WEINBERL *gets out his secret bottle and pours two*
drinks. They drink a silent toast. They look at each other.)

CHRISTOPHER: (*As* WEINBERL) 'I don't think you know my wife!'

(WEINBERL *splutters with pleasure.*)

WEINBERL: (*As* CHRISTOPHER) 'We want the best dinner in the
house and we want it now!'

(*They splutter joyfully and pummel each other about the*
shoulders.)

CHRISTOPHER: (*As* MISS BLUMENBLATT) 'Herr Sonders—you
know Herr Weinberl . . .'

WEINBERL: (*As* SONDERS) 'Marie—who is this impostor?'

(*But their joy evaporates almost immediately.* WEINBERL *sighs*
and reaches for the broom.)

Well . . . my chief sales assistant . . . Would you do me the
honour . . .

(*He bows and offers the broom which* CHRISTOPHER *takes.*

The street door opens to admit a small RAGAMUFFIN.)

RAGAMUFFIN: Are you the grocer, your eminence?

WEINBERL: I believe I am, sir.

RAGAMUFFIN: I understand you have an opening for an apprenticeship in the grocery trade.

WEINBERL: I believe I have, sir. The successful applicant will receive a thorough training in grocery, green grocery, charcuterie, weights and measures, stock-taking, window-dressing, debit, credit and personal hygiene. The hours are from dawn to dark and the pay is six guilders per month, less four guilders for board and lodging, one guilder for laundry, and one guilder put aside in your name against clothing and breakages. Would that be satisfactory?

RAGAMUFFIN: Yes, sir. I think that would be satisfactory.

WEINBERL: Have you any commercial experience?

RAGAMUFFIN: I have been chiefly holding horses' heads outside the Dog and Duck, sir. But I am my own master and can leave at any time.

WEINBERL: Christopher! Give him the broom!

RAGAMUFFIN: (*Joyfully*) Oh—thank you, sir!

(CHRISTOPHER *gives him the broom.*)

WEINBERL: You will find me a stern master but a fair one. I think I have some reputation in the mercantile world for—
(*Outside there is a roar of 'Weinberl' from* ZANGLER.)
(*Pause, gravely.*) Excuse me. I was away in Vienna yesterday and there are matters to discuss with my partner. (*He leaves.*)

RAGAMUFFIN: Vienna! Have you ever been to Vienna, sir?

CHRISTOPHER: Me? Oh yes. Good Lord. Of course.

RAGAMUFFIN: What is it like, sir?

CHRISTOPHER: (*Carelessly*) Vienna? Well it's . . .
(*Coming clean.*) wonderful!
(*The* RAGAMUFFIN *sweeps with furious delight.* CHRISTOPHER *watches him.*)

